I0609610

John Hall-Stevenson

**Crazy Tales**

John Hall-Stevenson

**Crazy Tales**

ISBN/EAN: 9783337344900

Printed in Europe, USA, Canada, Australia, Japan

Cover: Foto ©Andreas Hilbeck / pixelio.de

More available books at **www.hansebooks.com**

# C R A Z Y

# T A L E S.

*John Hall Stevenson*

Σκηνη πας ὁ Βιος και παιγνιον. η μαθε παιζειν
Την σπεδην μεταθεις η φερε τας οδυνας.

Life is a Farce, mere Children's Play,
 Go learn to model thine by theirs,
Go learn to trifle Life away,
 Or learn, to bear a Life of Cares.

 *J'abandonne l'exactitude*
  *Aux gens qui riment par métier ;*
 *D'autres font des vers par étude,*
  *J'en fais pour me defennüier.*

     GRESSET.

L O N D O N:
Printed in the YEAR MDCCLXII.

# Author's DEDICATION to Himself.

*Ever honoured and worthy Sir,*

ΠΑΝΤΩΝ δὲ μαλιϛ' αισχυιεο σαυτον. The reverence and refpect due to one's felf is the greateft of all, fays PYTHAGORAS : knowing how difficult it is to ferve two mafters, the Author is, and hopes he fhall always continue, accountable only to one.

There is fomething fo engaging in your fervice, that, though he can feldom do any thing entirely to your fatisfaction, yet he cannot find in his heart to be angry with you, or to wifh to change his dependence.

He is too fenfible of your difcernment to have any thoughts of wheedling you into an opinion of his performance; of the two he believes he could fooner prevail upon the world to be indulgent : the world has too much bufinefs upon its hands to be a fevere judge, or to be difficult to pleafe in trifles ; the world muft be amufed, but, like the *befoin d'aimer*, there is no neceffity for perfection to be one of the tranfient objects of its amufement.

All that the Author expects from you, is, that you will excufe his folly, and admit his apology for fuffering fuch trifles to appear in publick ; he can deal with other criticks well enough, if he is not condemned by you, being,

Ever honoured and worthy Sir,
with infinite attention,
your moft humble fervant,
A. S.

*Primum ego me illorum, dederim quibus effe poetas,*
*Excerpam numero----------*
     *Ex hoc ego fanus ab illis*
*Perniciem quæcunque ferunt ; mediocribus, et queis*
*Ignofcas, vitiis teneor-------ubi quid datur otî,*
*Illudo chartis. · Hoc eft mediocribus illis*
*Ex vitiis unum ; cui fi concedere nolis,*
*Multa poëtarum veniet manus, auxilio quæ*
*Sit mihi : nam multo plures fumus : ac veluti te*
*Judæi cogemus in hanc concedere turbam.*

By a *manœuvre* I conceive, &c. an ingenious Commentator may endeavour to charge the Author with impiety, as if he ridiculed Circumcifion; but, befides his being led into the mention of circumcifion by Horace, he only fpeaks of the operation, not of the inftitution ; that there is an effential difference between them, as well as degrees of nicety or ingenuity in the operative part, he will demonftrate.

No body can deny the ingenuity of his Coufin TRISTRAM's operation, if it had been produced by contrivance and ftudy, inftead of accident. If all children were circumcifed by the Shandean operation, by the fall of a fafh upon the forefkin, the difference in the operation would make no change in the inftitution ; as a Prieft would be a Prieft, whether he received the Spirit by a gentle tap, or obtained it by a more violent kind of electricity, by being knocked down. ·

So far from any impiety in the Author's propofition, we are bound to believe, if there had been any fafhes in the wildernefs, that the Shandean operation would have been preferred to the Mofaick, which was performed by two flint ftones; becaufe the Shandean is more expeditious, lefs painful, lefs dangerous, and confequently nicer and more ingenious. Q. E. D.

Upon a proper occafion the Author hopes he will be able to clear himfelf as fully of all intentional obfcenity, which may alfo be imputed to him by an ingenious Commentator.

*Triiblet, vol. iv. p.* 6. " On compofe pour imprimer, j'imprime pour compofer. Si en compofant je n'avois pas le but de l'impreffion, mon travail ne féroit pas affez animé pour me fauver de l'ennui, quelqu'eut été le fort de mes Effais, &c. J'en avois deja retiré, avant de les publier, un fruit affez precieux que le fuccès même. Ils m'avoient longtems occupé fans trop m'appliquer."

THE

# Author's APOLOGY to Himself.

FREE from all pernicious vice
　　Yet not fo fcrupuloufly good,
To want a comfortable fpice,
　　To warm a fober Chriftian's blood.

The fin of Harlotry and-Keeping,
　　Is that which I can leaft excufe,
That of cohabiting and fleeping,
　　With an abandon'd common Mufe.

More like a Mufe's toad-eater;
　　A trollop with a flippant air,
Without one amiable feature,
　　Or any graces to her fhare.

You tell me, if I needs muft print,
　　You'll not oppofe my foolifh will,
And bid me take a fober hint
　　From fober folks at Strawberry Hill.

Stand forth like them, produce yourfelf,
　　Be elegantly bound and letter'd;
Be wife, like them, nor quit your fhelf,
　　But there remain, for ever fetter'd.

I do

I do not print to get a name;
   As TRUBLET fays, I am none of thofe;
I only print, becaufe my aim
   Is happinefs, whilft I compofe:
Compofing gives us no delight,
Unlefs we mean to publifh what we write.

Scribbling, like Praying's, an employment,
   In which you would think yourfelf a bubble,
Without fome profpect of enjoyment,
   And fatisfaction for your trouble;
And though your hopes at laft prove vain,
If you have been amus'd, 'twas fo much gain.

If you ftill teaze me, and perfift
   That publifhing fhews a vain heart,
The Songfters upon DODSLEY's lift
   Shall be call'd in to take my part.

And as they ftrip a lad quite bare,
   After they've coax'd him from his play,
Then lay him down, and cut and pare
   All his impediments away:

And as the lad without his leave
   Is made an excellent Mufician,
By a manœuvre I conceive
   As nice as TRISTRAM's Circumcifion:

                          So

So tho' you only juſt can ſcrape
   Among the Fidlers of the Nine,
They'll make you drunker than an ape,
   And make you think you fiddle fine.

**PROLOGUE**

# PROLOGUE

## TO THE

## CRAZY TALES.

*Quod petis hic est,*
*Eſt Ulubris animus ſi te non deficit æquis.*

THERE is a Caſtle in the North,
 Seated upon a ſwampy clay,
 At preſent but of little worth,
In former times it had its day.

This antient Caſtle is call'd CRAZY,
 Whoſe mould'ring walls a moat environs,
Which moat goes heavily and lazy.
 Like a poor priſoner in irons.

Many a time I've ſtood and thought,
 Seeing the boat upon this ditch,
It look'd as if it had been brought
 For the amuſement of a Witch,
To ſail amongſt applauding frogs,
With water-rats, dead cats and dogs.

The

The boat fo leaky is and old,
 That if you're fanciful and merry,
You may conceive, without being told,
 That it refembles Charon's wherry.

A turrit alfo you may note,
 Its glory vanifh'd like a dream,
Transform'd, into a pigeon-coat,
 Nodding befide the fleepy ftream.

 —ence, by fteps with mofs o'ergrown,
 —mount upon a terrace high,
 —here ftands that heavy pile of ftone,
 Irregular and all awry.

If many a buttrefs did not reach,
 A kind, and falutary hand,
Did not encourage, and befeech,
 The terrace and the houfe to ftand,
Left to themfelves and at a lofs;
They'd tumble down, into the fofs.

Over the Caftle hangs a tow'r,
Threatning deftruction ev'ry hour,
Where owls, and bats, and the jackdaw,
 Their Vefpers and their Sabbath keep,
All night fcream horribly, and caw,
 And fnore all day, in horrid fleep.

Oft at the quarrels and the noife
Of fcolding maids or idle boys;

Myriads

Myriads of rooks rife up and fly,
  Like legions of damn'd fouls,
    As black as coals,
That foul and darken all the fky.

With wood the Caftle is furrounded,
  Except an opening to a Peak,
Where the beholder ftands confounded,
  At fuch a fcene of mountains bleak;

    Where nothing goes,
  Except fome folitary pewet,
    And carrion crows,
That feem fincerely to rue it,
That look as if they had been banifh'd,
And had been fentenc'd to be famifh'd.

    Where nothing grows,
    So keen it blows,
Save here and there a gracelefs fir,
  From Scotland, with its kindred fled,
That moves its arms, and makes a ftir,
  And toffes its fantaftick head,
That feems to make a noife and cry,
Only for want of company.

So a Scotch Minifter in pulpit,
  Is wrought by his gefticulation,
'Till he is taken with a dull fit,
  Peculiar to that vocation.

He

He cries, and throws about his fnivel,
 Their hearts are harder than the flint,
They let him weep alone, and drivel,
 For not a foul will take the hint.

In this retreat, whilom fo fweet,
 Once TRISTRAM and his Coufin dwelt,
They talk of CRAZY when they meet,
 As if their tender hearts would melt.

Confounded in Time's common urn,
 With Harlots, Minifters, and Kings,
O could fuch fcenes again return!
 Like thofe infipid common things!

Many a grievous, heavy heart,
 To CRAZY Caftle would repair,
That grew, from dragging like a cart,
 Elaftick and as light as air.

Some fell to fiddling, fome to fluting,
 Some to fhooting, fome to fifhing,
Others to pifhing and difputing,
 Or to computing by wifhing.

And in the evening when they met,
 To think on't always does me good,
There never met a jollier fet,
 Either before, or fince the Flood.

At long as CRAZY Caftle lafts,
   Their Tales will never be forgot;
And CRAZY may ftand many blafts,
   And better caftles go to pot.

ANTONY, Lord of CRAZY Caftle,
   Neither a fifher, nor a fhooter,
No man's, but any woman's vaffal,
   If he could find a way to fuit her ;
Collected all their Tales into a book,
Which you may fee if you go there to look.

ANTO-

# ANTONY's TALE:

## OR THE

## Boarding-School TALE.

### TALE I.

LUCY was not like other laffes,
　　From twelve her breafts fwell'd in a trice,
Firft they were like two cupping-glaffes,
　　Then like two peaches made of ice,

With fwimming eyes and golden locks,
　　Golden embroidery and fringe,
Like an ivory or Drefden box,
　　Mounted with golden lips and hinge,

Or like the Glory round the head,
　　Of virgin Saints weeping and pale,
When they are facrific'd, and led
　　To martyrdom, or to a male.

Or as a comet's golden tale is;
　　Or like the undulating light
Of the aurora borealis,
　　In a ferene autumnal night.

It

It is a fhame, fays her Mamma,
To fee a child with bib and apron,
   At BARE thirteen, an age fo RAW,
Grown and furnifh'd like a matron.

   But if it was a Burning Shame,
   LUCY was not at all to blame,
But they, who in her compofition,
   Infus'd that warmth which was the caufe
Of fuch exuberant nutrition,
   The work of vegetative laws.

'Twas at the age I mention'd,
   Upon a very flight offence,
LUCY was condemn'd and penfion'd,
   Againft all equity and fenfe,
Within a Boarding-fchool's detefted walls,
   Doom'd to feel all its rigours, all its thralls,

To endure the hunger and the chidings!
   To feel the longings and the watchings!
To dread the ftealings and the hidings!
   To bear the quarrels and the fcratchings!

And then fuch billings, and fuch cooings!
   Such Mifs-demeanours and excufes!
Such Mifs-takes, and fuch Mifs-doings!
   And fuch Mifs-fortunes and abufes!

                  There

There was a Captain of the Guards,
  A famous Knight of Arthur's table,
Expert in woman, vers'd in cards,
  A brother of the Turf and Stable.

He had such a command of features,
  And was so droll and full of sport,
He could take off all the queer creatures,
  And oddities of Arthur's Court.

Set Arthur's Worthies in a row,
  So very comical a Knight,
You could not single out and shew,
  Nor one that gave so much delight.

One day whilst our Knight was busy,
  Extremely busy with her Mother,
Lucy had run 'till she was dizzy,
  About the Garden with her brother.

The Captain's bus'nefs being done,
  He saunter'd up and down the Garden,
As if he had neither lost nor won,
  As if he did not care a farthing.

Yet his attention was profound,
  Observing Lucy grown so tall;
Contemplating her breasts as round,
  And springy as a tennis ball.

The

The fight, indeed, was quite bewitching,
　I think I fee him whilft I'm fcribbling,
Mouth watering, and fingers itching,
　To be both fingering and nibbling.

To gratify the two young chicks,
　He roll'd his eyes, and acted Punch;
Playing a thoufand monkey tricks,
　Making his back a perfect bunch.

With many a filthy flobbering kifs,
　Courting in Punch's fqueaking tone,
And wriggling and embracing Mifs,
　As Punch embraces his wife Joan.

And how to imitate a breaft,
　The Captain faid that Mifs had plac'd,
Swelling on each fide of her cheft,
　Two little dumplings made of pafte;
At which Punch gap'd, and fwore an oath,
That he would take and eat them both.

On Lucy's neck the hungry fpark
　Hung fix'd, like an envenom'd fnake,
Leaving a deep indented mark,
　Which her Mamma could not miftake;
For which irregular proceeding,
Lucy was fent to ftudy breeding.

LUCY was angry with good caufe,
  For fhe had feen in former days,
Necks very like her own Mamma's,
  Without a handkerchief or ftays,

It might be fuller and more nourifh'd,
  And yet a neck, not more inviting,
LUCY had feen it fcrawl'd and flourifh'd
  Both with marks, and with hand-writing.

LUCY, tho' watchful and awake,
  And mighty curious to know;
Perhaps was under a miftake,
  What fhe had feen was long ago:

Would it not make one almoft wild,
  If it was not fo very common;
To fee one punifh'd like a child,
  Only for acting like a woman?
To fee the moment after, may be,
Her mother acting like a baby.

Sent to a Governefs of fpirit,
  LUCY was watch'd from head to foot,
Juft like a rabbit with a ferret,
  For ever at the rabbit's fcut.
All the whole day in durance kept,
At night the Governefs with LUCY flept.

                                    But

But Lucy neither flept, nor flumber'd,
  She tofs'd; and tumbled all the night;
Her fpirits were fo much encumber'd,
  And flurry'd by the Captain's bite.

Whether their poifon they impart,
  By teeth, or nails, or by a fting,
There is a virtue in fome part,
  Of every poifonous thing.

Tho' the experiment fhould fright her,
  Enough to throw her in a fit,
Lucy muft apply the biter,
  Unto the poifon'd-part that's bit.

Granted; but how could fhe contrive
  To bring fo hard a point to bear?
'Twould puzzle any wit alive,
  That had not a great deal to fpare.

There's a remark, 'twas made long finee,
Machiavell made it for his Prince;
" A Prince, fays he, completely cruel,
  " Throughout inexorably bad,
" Is an ineftimable jewel,
  " Seldom or never to be had."

        Tho'

Tho' cruel often, and hard-hearted,
   Lucy's Mamma, at laft, could not withftand,
She gave her blefling when they parted,
   And flipp'd a guinea into Lucy's hand.

With one poor guinea Lucy bought
   All that the Wife, the Rich, and Great,
So frequently in vain have fought,
   Both in the world and their retreat :

No Potentate could ever buy it,
   Nor any child of Power and Wealth,
Tranquillity or mental Quiet,
   With Liberty, Content, and Health.

Lucy conducted her affairs,
   So circumfpectly, and fo fnug,
By bribes fhe gain'd a friend down ftairs,
   And made a purchafe of a drug,
Which drug is, in the vulgar tongue,
Commonly call'd, The Devil's Dung.

Within the lining of her gown,
   In two fmall bags under each arm,
She beat and fow'd it nicely down,
   As if fhe had fow'd down a charm.

The exhalation was fo ftrong
　From every part of Lucy's cloaths,
The Miffes, as fhe pafs'd along,
　Brufhed away, and held their nofe.

By far the greateft part prefum'd,
　That it was owing to her hair,
Others prefum'd fhe was perfum'd,
　From being rotten as a pear.

The fcent fo violent was grown,
　Her Governefs was forc'd to yield,
The room, the maid, were all her own,
　Arms, tents, and baggage, and the field.

# ODE to VENUS.

O VENUS, awful Sovereign of the Spring,
Could I like thy Lucretius fing,
Here would I paufe, thy wonders to relate!
　Here would I paufe, to hymn thy praife,
In adamantine words, ftronger than Fate,
　And everlafting as his lays!

O'er feas and deferts, undifmay'd,
　Strengthen'd by thy infpiring breath,
The timorous and bafhful maid,
　Faces both Infamy and Death.

Driven

Driven by thy incens'd divinity,
   Confounding equity and truth,
Order and rank, and confanguinity,
   And loathfome age and blooming youth.

Behold the frantick paffion how it burns,
   Like a wild beaft breaks every tie,
Laughs at the Prieft; the Legiflator fpurns,
   And gives both heav'n and earth the lie!

Let youth and infolence alone,
   Provoke thy vengeance every hour;
But O! fpare thofe that know, that own,
   Adore, and tremble at thy power.

With thy propitious doves defcend,
   And hear the tender virgin's fighs,
The humble and the meek defend,
   And bid the proftrate fuppliant rife.

———

By VENUS LUCY, was protected,
Nothing was hurry'd, or neglected,
The Miffes, tho' fhe was quite well,
   Tofs'd up their nofes, full of airs,
Tho' LUCY now had no one fmell,
   That was not pleafanter than theirs.

For

For a whole winter, every night
   (Which made the wench grow monſtrous thin)
'Till the war call'd him out to fight,
   Had Susan let the Captain in,

Scarce had he left his native coaſt,
   'Till Lucy ſummon'd home, became
A celebrated London toaſt,
   And the firſt favourite of Fame.

Lucy was follow'd by a Peer,
   But all his arts could not trepan her,
After a ſiege of a whole year,
   My Lord was forc'd to change his manner;
So, like a wife and virtuous girl,
Lucy, at laſt, was marry'd to an Earl.

# My COUSIN's TALE

### OF

# A COCK and a BULL.

### TALE II.

AT CAMBRIDGE many years ago,
   In JESUS, was a Walnut-tree;
The only thing, it had to fhew,
   The only thing, folks went to fee.

Being of fuch a fize and mafs,
   And growing in fo wife a College,
I wonder how it came to pafs,
   It was not call'd the Tree of Knowledge.

Indeed, if you attempt to run,
   (The air fo heavy is, and muddy)
Any great length beyond a pun,
   You'll be obliged to fweat and ftudy.

This is the reafon 'tis fo good for tificks,
   And will account, why no one foph,
   No Fellow, ever could hit off,
To call this Tree, the Tree of Metaphyficks.

Tho'

Tho', in the midſt of the quadrangle,
   They ev'ry one were taught their trade;
They ev'ry one were taught to wrangle,
   Beneath its ſcientifick ſhade.

It overſhadow'd ev'ry room,
   And conſequently, more or leſs,
Forc'd ev'ry brain, in ſuch a gloom,
   To grope its way, and go by gueſs.

For ever going round about;
   For that which lies before your noſe,
And when you come to find it out,
   It is not like what you ſuppoſe.

So have I often ſeen in fogs,
   A may-pole taken for a ſteeple;
Chriſtians oft miſtook for hogs,
   Horſes ta'en for Chriſtian people.

This ſtroke upon my tender brain
   Remains, I doubt, impreſs'd for ever,
For to this day, when with much pain,
   I try to think ſtrait on, and clever,
I ſidle out again, and ſtrike
   Into the beautiful oblique.

D

Therefore, I have no one notion,
 That is not form'd, like the defigning
Of the periftaltick motion ;
 Vermicular ; twifting and twining ;
  Going to work
Juft like a bottle-fkrew upon a cork.

This obliquity of thinking
 I cur'd, formerly, by Logick,
And a habitude of drinking,
 Infufions pædagogick.

The cure is worfe than the difeafe,
 'Tis juft like drinking fo much gall ;
So I keep thinking at my eafe ;
 That is, I never think at all.

Thus a prefuming Mifs defigns,
 Quite over-whelm'd with foolifh pride,
She drops her paper with black lines,
 And trufts herfelf without a guide.

No longer kept within due bounds,
 For any thing that you can fay,
Her letters like unruly hounds,
 Running all a different way ;
No longer writes as heretofore,
But writes awry both now and ever more.

But

But, *a propos*, of bottle-ſkrews,
 You've ſeen a Parſon at a table,
Whoſe buſineſs was to read the news,
 And draw a cork, if he was able.

And do remember, I dare ſay,
 The fooliſh figure that he makes,
When the cork will not come away,
 For all the pains the Parſon takes.

By bit and bit he makes it come,
 'Till he is forc'd againſt his will,
To puſh it forward with his thumb;
 He has conducted it ſo ill.

Thus with my head have I been here,
 Screwing to get at what I wanted:
That you might have a Tale as clear
 And bright, as if it was decanted.
But as your time and patience are ſo ſhort,
I'll try to get at it in any ſort.

  I N Italy there is a town,
  Anciently of great renown;
Call'd, by the Volſcians, Privernum;
 A fortreſs againſt the Romans,
Maintain'd, becauſe it did concern 'em,
 Spite of Rome, and all her omens;
  But to their coſt,
At the long run their town was loſt.

   D 2      Whether

Whether 'twas forc'd or did surrender,
  You never need, my dear Sir, know,
Provided you will but remember,
  Privernum signifies Piperno.


Close by the Francifcan Friars,
  There liv'd a Saint, as all declare,
All the world cannot be liars,
  Which Saint wrought miracles by pray'r.


Her life so holy was, and pure,
  Her pray'rs, at all times they believe,
Could heirs or heiresses secure,
  And make the barren womb conceive.


Which was a safe expedient,
  And wonderful convenient :
For there was not a barren womb,
    That might not try,
Going between Naples and Rome,
    As she pass'd by.


My story will not be the worse,
  If you'll reflect with patience,
Upon the constant intercourse
  Between the neighbour nations.


It

It is fo great, that I dare fay,
    The Saint could have but little eafe,
She muft have been both night and day,
    Continually on her knees.

For I can prove it very clear,
    That many of thofe wombs are barren,
Which wombs, were they tranfplanted here,
    Would breed like rabbits in a warren.

Near Terracina, once call'd Anxur,
    There is a place call'd Bofco Folto,
A caftle ftanding on a bank, Sir,
    The feat of the Marchefe STOLTO.

In hiftory you all have read,
    Moft of you have, I'm pretty fure,
How on that road there is no bed,
    Nor any inn, you can endure.

For STOLTO I had got a letter,
    From my good friend, Prince MALA-FEDE,
And from the Princefs a much better,
    Wrote to his Excellency's Lady.

The Marquis is advanc'd in years,
    And dries you fo, there's no efcaping,
The merrieft, when he appears,
    Yawn, and fet the reft a gaping,

*Seccare*

*Seccare* is a word of fun ;
  It means to dry, as you may find,
Not like the fire, or like the fun,
  But like a cold unpleafant wind.

But fhe is perfectly well bred ;
  Neither too forward, nor too fhy :
I never did, in any head,
  In all my life, fee fuch an-eye;

Nor fuch a head on any fhoulders;
  Nor fuch a neck, with fuch a fwell,
  That could prefent itfelf fo well,
To all the critical beholders.

Four years the Marquis was hum-drumming,
  In that fame place, with his bed-fellow,
Waiting for the happy coming
  Of a young Marquis, a.STOLTELLO.

As foon as ever he arrives,
  The family is to be fent to
The Cardinal at Benevento,
  For the remainder of their lives.

The Cardinal is STOLTO's nephew,
  His age is only twenty-feven ;
And of that age there are but few,
  Who think, like him, of nought but Heav'n.

His

His aunt will manage and take care
  Of all the Cardinal's affairs,
STOLTELLO is to be his heir,
  When he has finiſh'd all his prayers.


STOLTO may live as he thinks good,
  His life delightfully will run,
Between his caſtle in the wood,
  His wife, his nephew, and his ſon.


And yet according to Fame's trumpet,
  Who very ſeldom trumpets right,
His wife was reckon'd a great ſtrumpet,
  His nephew a great hypocrite.


I don't believe a word of that,
The world will talk, and let it chat:
You cannot think her in the wrong,
  To grow quite weary of the place,
She thought STOLTELLO ſtaid ſo long,
  He was aſham'd to ſhew his face.


STOLTO had heard the Holy Maid
  Always cry'd up both far and near,
And he believ'd ſhe could perſuade
  His ſon STOLTELLO to appear.

Con-

Confidering what time was paft,
   How they had try'd, and better try'd,
STOLTO advis'd his wife at laft,
   To go and be fecundify'd.

The Marquis told me the whole ftory,
   Which he had from the Marchefina,
And it is fo much to her glory;
   'Tis all the talk of Terracina.

The very night that fhe came back,
   He was in fuch a fifting cue;
He almoft put her to the rack,
   'Till fhe difcover'd all fhe knew.

Firft his acknowledgment being paid,
   A pepper-cornifh kind of due;
As they were laid, compos'd and ftaid,
   She told him juft as I tell you:

Before the Marchionefs fets out,
   'Tis proper, on reflection,
To obviate a certain doubt,
   That looks like an objection.

Here, becaufe they know no better,
   The fnarlers think they've found a Bone;
They think the Marquis would not let her
   Go fuch an errand all alone.

                    A Lady,

A Lady, you muſt underſtand,
   That viſits, to fulfil HER vows,
A holy houſe, or holy land,
   Commonly goes without her ſpouſe.

And ſo, by keeping herſelf ſtill,
   Quiet and ſober in her bed,
She never thinks of any ill,
   Nothing unclean enters her head.

You're ſatisfy'd your doubt was weak,
And now the Marchioneſs may ſpeak.
As you foretold, before I went,
   The Saint was ſo engag'd, and watch'd,
That a whole week and more was ſpent,
   Before my buſ'neſs was diſpatch'd.

Indeed you would have greatly pity'd,
   If you had ſeen me but, my Dear;
Howe'er, at laſt, I was admitted,
   And what I met with you ſhall hear.

The Saint and I ſat on a bench;
   Before us, on a couch there lay,
A pretty little naked wench,
   That minded nothing but her play.

E

Her

Her play, was playing with a moufe,
That popp'd its head in, went and came,
And neftled in its little houfe,
It was fo docible and tame.

Guefs where the moufe had found a bower?
You are fo dull, it is a fhame;
You cannot guefs in half an hour,
I'll lay your hand upon the fame.

Thefe, cry'd the Saint, are all ideal,
Vifions all, and nothing real,
Yet they will animate your blood,
And rouze and warm the pregnant pow'rs,
Juft like the ling'ring fickly bud,
Open'd by fructifying fhow'rs.

If you are violently heated,
Remember, in your greateft needs,
Your Ave Mary be repeated,
'Till you have gone thro' all your Beads:
Take heed, they're going to begin,
I fee the vifions coming in.

Firft came a Cock, and then a Bull,
And then a Heifer and a Hen;
'Till they had got their bellies full,
On and off, and on again.

And

And then I fpy'd a foolifh Filly,
   That was reduc'd to a ftrange pafs,
Languifhing, and looking filly,
   At the propofals of an Afs.

I turn'd about and faw a fight,
   Which was a fight I could not bear,
A filthy Horfe, with all his might,
   Gallanting with a filthy Mare.

And lo! there came a dozen Priefts!
   And all the Priefts fhaven and fhorn!
And they were like a dozen beafts,
   Naked as ever they were born:
     And they pafs'd on,
     One by one,
Ev'ry one with an exalted horn.

Then they drew up and ftood a while,
     In rank and file,
And after, march'd off the parade,
     One by one,
     Falling upon,
The miferable, naked Maid.

Nothing could equal my furprize,
   To fee her go thro' great and fmall!
And after that, to fee her rife,
   And turn the joke upon them all!

And I kept praying ftill and counting,
  In a prodigious fret and heat,
And fhe fucceffively kept mounting, .
  And always kept a fteady feat.

'Till having finifh'd her career,
  The Priefts were terribly perplex'd,
They could not tell which way to fteer,
  Nor where about to fettle next.

Brother was running after Brother,
Turning their horns againft each other,
The Holy Maid cry'd out aloud,
  Heaven deliver us from fin :
And I turn'd up my eyes and bow'd,
  And faid Amen within :
  The inftant that I fpoke,
The vifions vanifh'd into fmoke.

Now, faid the Marchionefs, and fmil'd;
  I'll give a penny for your thought;
I'll lay, you think, if we've a child,
  STOLTELLO will be dearly bought?

———

Accordingly the Marquis fwore,
  That very night he did a feat,
Which he had feldom done before,
  That night he ran a fecond heat.

And from that night computing fair,
      She had conceiv'd,
About five months when I was there,
As both the Marchionefs and he believ'd.

For four months after I repafs'd,
   Calling again, to avoid thofe inns,
     And found her brought to-bed, at laft,
        Of twins,
So ftout, the brothers might have pafs'd for
   POLLUX and CASTOR.

And fo, at laft, his coft and toil,
   The Marquis was oblig'd to own,
Were laid out on a grateful foil,
   At laft, he reap'd as he had fown.

# MISS in her TEENS:
## Captain SHADOW's TALE.

### TALE III.

MISS MOLLY was almoſt fourteen,
   Her Couſin DICK a year older,
The diff'rence of a year between,
Was very eaſy to be ſeen,
For DICK was grown a year bolder.

Tho' he was grown bolder and braver,
   MOLLY grew baſhfuller and ſhier,
So ſerious, and ſo much graver,
   She hardly would let DICK come nigh her.

The year before, upon no ſcore,
   Would DICK be caught in ſuch a trick,
   As either peeping thro' a nick,
Or thro' the key-hole of a door.

The year before Miſs had no fears,
   And there was no ſuch thing as ſquealing,
And DICK had neither eyes nor ears,
   Neither taſte, nor ſmell, nor feeling.

Until

Until this year, as I have heard,
  DICK was unlucky, but not rude;
  And MOLLY so far from a prude,
'Till now her door was never barr'd.


One afternoon Mamma rode out,
  Papa was laid up in the gout,
Well, and what became of MOLLY?
  If she had taken her to ride,
  She should have been confin'd and try'd,
For flagrant and wilful folly.


When they are let out of the cage,
  Without confideration,
All children of a certain age,
  Are giv'n to obfervation.


Their judgment's fo exceeding weak
  Their fancy fo exceeding ftrong,
That you can neither act nor fpeak,
  They are fo apt to take things wrong.


So neither Mifs, nor DICK the fapling,
        With Madam rides,
She is attended by the Chaplain
        And none befides.

Which

Which of the two were better pleas'd,
   Is difficult to fay, I own,
Mifs and Papa had been fo teaz'd,
   They both were pleas'd to be alone.

Up to her chamber MOLLY's flown,
   Faft bolted is her chamber door,
So cautious the damfel's grown,
   From what Mifs MOLLY was before.

Ever fince DICK began to pry,
   Ever fince MOLLY caft her frock,
She never ventures to rely
   On the protection of a lock.

MOLLY fufpects her coufin DICK,
   Her coufin DICK's fo plaguy fly,
That lock, or any lock can pick,
   That DICK has any mind to try.

DICK pick the lock ! it could not be,
   If MOLLY only had the fenfe,
As foon as fhe had turn'd the key,
   Not to have taken it from thence.

MOLLY would gladly have compounded,
   If DICK would let her fcape fo cheap,
Whenever MOLLY was impounded,
   She left that hole for DICK to peep.

                           She

She knew there was no keeping,
　　Her coufin DICK from peeping :
For fure as ever you're alive,
　　Either with gimlet or fkewer,
Her coufin RICHARD would contrive
　　To bore a hole, fomewhere, to view her.

For fome particular affair,
　　That MOLLY had in agitation,
She did not at that juncture care,
　　To be expos'd to fpeculation.

She clap'd a fire-fkreen to the hole,
　　To hinder coufin DICK from fpying;
Little imagining, poor foul,
　　That DICK was in her clofet lying.

The room, as you have heard me tell,
　　At all times had been MOLLY's own,
The clofet was a citadel
　　Of a late date, to awe the town.

Mamma had thought upon the cafe,
　　And thinking made her more afraid,
A clofet was a dangerous place
　　For ftratagem and ambufcade;
So the room ftill to Mifs remains,
The fort to Mamma appertains.

F

The

The key that opens this fame fort,
Mamma had loft, in a ftrange fort,
In riding out, the key fhe loft;
    And it was found by DICK at play,
Upon the fpot where it was tofs'd,
    Upon a heap of new made hay.

Her pad, I fancy, for my part,
Is badly broke, and apt to ftart:
And by a fudden jirk or fpring,
Or fwing, or fome fuch thing;
    Out flew the key, as if a ftone
            Had flown,
    Out of a fling.

Pray, where was Mifs's great neglect?
    Where was her indifcretion?
This treach'rous key could fhe fufpect
    To be in DICK's poffeffion?

She was fo deliberate and cool,
    Each nook and cranny fhe furvey'd;
She even examin'd the clofe-ftool,
    But DICK was in the clofet laid.

Whate'er he faw, DICK never told,
    And that is much for one fo young,
When people that are twice as old,
    Have twice as indifcreet a tongue.

It muſt be ſomething curious,
  Some extraordinary matter,
DICK ſtar'd and look'd ſo furious,
  When he bounc'd out and flew at her.

Tho' ſhe was cruelly betray'd,
  DICK made up matters very ſoon,
MOLLY was reconcil'd, DICK ſtay'd
  And ſpent a pleaſant afternoon.

The point was long, and well debated,
  But DICK ſo ſolemnly proteſted,
By MOLLY he was reinſtated,    .
  And with the key fairly inveſted.    ..

Mamma perceiv'd the key was ſtray'd,
  And ſent the Chaplain out to look,
'Twas not for that ſhe was diſmay'd,
  But ſhe had loſt her pocket-book.

He found the book, which was the beſt;
  As to the key, the careful mother,
Before ſhe laid her head to reſt,
  Sent and beſpoke juſt ſuch another.

'Twas well, ſhe let the lock remain;
  Had it been chang'd on his report,
It would have caus'd infinite pain,
  And ſpoil'd a deal of harmleſs ſport.

                    In

In a fhort time MOLLY grew fick,
  Every day ficker and ficker,
MOLLY's complaints came very thick,
  Every day thicker and thicker.
She was advis'd to change the air,
She did, but no-body knows where.

MOLLY came home a different thing,
  Both in her fhape and every feature,
From what fhe went away in fpring,
  You never faw a virgin fweeter.

'Squire NODDY coming from his travels,
  By MOLLY is a captive led,
He to her Sire his mind unravels,
  Her Sire confents, and MOLLY's wed.

It is fix years that 'Squire NODDY
Has had the care of MOLLY's body;
  And they have children half a dozen ;
But what is very odd is this,
That none of all the fix fhould mifs,
  But every one be like her coufin.

# ZACHARY's TALE;

## OR THE

# SUSPICIOUS HUSBAND Cured.

The Actors in this Dramatick Tale, are

| | |
|---|---|
| The Suspicious Husband, | ANGRAVALLE. |
| His Wife, | BINDOCCHIA. |
| Her Friend, | PAULINA. |
| Her Husband's Friend, | NICENO. |

Scene NAPLES.

PART the FIRST.

# Z. M. Efquire,

A living Monument,
Of the Friendfhip and Generofity of the Great;
After an Intimacy of thirty Years,
With moft of the great Perfonages of thefe Kingdoms,
Who did him the Honour to affift him,
In the laborious Work,
Of getting to the far End of a great Fortune,
Thefe his Noble Friends,
From Gratitude for the many happy Days and Nights
Enjoy'd by his Means,
Exalted him, through their Influence,
In the forty-feventh year of his Age,
To an Enfigncy;
Which he actually enjoys at prefent
In GIBRALTAR.

# ODE to ZACHARY.

*Omnis Ariſtippum decuit, color, et modus, et res—*
*Nunc in Ariſtippi furtim præcepta relabor,*
*Et mihi res, non me rebus ſubmittere conor—.*

WHAT ſober heads haſt thou made ake?
　　How many haſt thou kept from nodding?
How many wife-ones, for thy fake,
　　Have flown to thee, and left off plodding?

Thou wouldſt, altho' the grave-ones ſhake
　　Their ſolemn locks, and ſtrike one mute,
As ſoon be in the infernal lake,
　　As in the place of P--T or B--TE;

Whoſe heads inceſſantly ſend forth
　　Projects, with glitt'ring trains, like ſquibs,
And ſcatter, through the South and North,
　　Vollies of Miniſterial Fibs.

Aſleep, down precipices hurry'd,
　　Or, like PROMETHEUS chain'd to rocks—
By vulturs gnaw'd, or monſters worry'd,
　　Hell-hounds, whoſe cry is, *Dei Vox*—

Or,

Or, victims to a heavier curfe,
  They dream they're dup'd, and fall unpity'd;
To fall a dupe, is ten times worfe,
  Than to be worried and dewitted.

Philofophy and Grace is thine,
  Not fpiritual Grace, but fprightly;
Infpir'd by the God of Wine,
  Like old ANACREON nightly.

That Light divine, that heav'nly Grace,
  I fear, alas! thou wouldft not chufe;
That fhines and blackens WHITFIELD's face,
  Like the japan upon his fhoes.

Whether thy Grace from Heav'n defcends,
  Or rifes from the earth below,
Oft haft thou rais'd thy helplefs friends,
  Oft giv'n thy purfe unto thy foe---

Who gives his foe his purfe outright,
  Shews plain, if I have any fkill,
Not only that he bears no fpite,
  But that he bears him a good will.

And alfo, is perhaps as meek,
  And is as little of a bite,
As he who only gives his cheek
  (For LESLY gives nought elfe) to fmite:

Or

Or WHITFIELD emptying the pockets
   Of whores, and bawds, and gaping throngs;
Turning his eyes out of their fockets,
   Singing and felling DAVID's fongs.

Now thou art gone, where can I find
   Spirit and eafe above controul,
Serenity and health of mind,
   And gaiety and ftrength of foul ?
Precepts I find, examples none,
And guides as blind as a guide-ftone.

The fportive Mufe is my Phyfician,
   To cure the folly, and the madnefs,
Of Pride, of Envy, and Ambition;
   Of Spleen, and melancholy Sadnefs.

Soon as I touch the jocund lyre,
   That inftant, driven from their feat,
The dæmons of the mind retire,
   And go and perfecute the Great.

O! may their torments never ceafe,
   May they be fcourg'd both night and day,
'Till they have brought thee back in peace,
   And then, like thee, may they be ever gay!

*This*

*This is so long a Tale, that* ZACHARY *thought it would be better divided into Two Parts.*

BANDELLO lived in the fixteenth century, in high reputation for his wit, and correfponded with all the great men of that age : He retired into France upon the taking of Milan by the Spaniards, at which time all his papers were burnt: In 1551 he was made Bifhop of Agen in France, where his Novels were firft publifhed.

Outcries againft writings, compofed with no worfe intention than to promote good-humour and chearfulnefs, by fighting againft the *Tædium Vitæ,* were referved for an age of refined hypocrify. There ought to be a great diftinction between obfcenity, evidently defigned to inflame the paffions, and a ludicrous liberty, which is frequently neceffary to fhew the true ridicule of hypocritical characters, which can give offence to none, but fuch as are afraid of every thing that has a tendency to unmafking.

The fecond part of this Tale is upon a different plan from BANDELLO'S: ZACHARY has told the Bifhop's Tale with more modefty than the Bifhop, and I think the cataftrophe is more natural. The beft edition of BANDELLO is printed at Lucca in 1554, and reprinted in London, in three volumes, quarto, 1740.

# ZACHARY'S TALE.

## TALE IV.

HOW oft has BOCCACE been tranſlated
    And blunder'd,
And JEAN FONTAINE aſſaſſinated,
    And plunder'd :
Where is the land where BOCCACE and FONTAINE
Have not in effigy been ſlain ?

FONTAINE they imitate and turn,
    BOCCACE they repreſent and render,
Juſt as the figures made to burn,
    Are like the Pope and the Pretender.

Why mayn't BANDELLO have a rap ?
    Why mayn't I imitate BANDELLO ?
There never was a Prelate's cap
    Beſtow'd upon a droller fellow ?

Like TRISTRAM, in mirth delighting ;
    Like TRISTRAM, a pleaſant Writer ;
Like his, I hope, that TRISTRAM's writing
    Will be rewarded with a Mitre.

There was a Knight, ſays our Biſhop,
    A Knight from Aragon in Spain,
So jealous, that you cannot fiſh up
    His like and paragon again :

G 2

He

He ſerv'd ALPHONSUS many years,
   Both in the wars and in affairs of State,
And fell in love up to the ears,
   And would not give it up at any rate.
By bribes and flattery he won
Father, mother, daughter, and ſon.


And yet he ſerenaded, ſigh'd,
   And was long doubtful of his doom,
Before he gain'd his lovely Bride,
   With all the rights of a Bridegroom.


And after that, they tell us,
That in leſs time than you would think,
   He grew ſo plaguy jealous,
He could not ſleep o'nights a wink.


He was not jealous, ſays the Tale,
   All the time he was in training;
'Twas not 'till he began to fail,
   And to fall off, by over-ſtraining.


As ſoon as ever he train'd off,
   The nights ſhe paſs'd can ſcarce be told;
All night he could do nought but cough,
   Torment, and tantalize, and ſcold.


BINDOCCHIA

BINDOCCHIA was lively and alert,
　And had no notion of a bridle,
She requir'd one, not only more expert,
　But one as active as her spouse was idle.

Now ANGRAVALLE knew all this,
　As well as either you or I,
When he thought proper to difmifs
　Thofe, on whofe help he might rely.

He turn'd off men and maids,
　　All together;
　　Birds of a feather;
Rogues, and intriguing jades;
All but a fellow with a furly look,
Gard'ner, butler, groom, and cook:

And, to cut off all hopes to come,
　From an intriguing maid at leaft,
He pick'd up one both deaf and dumb,
　And neither fit for man nor beaft---

Befides, he had fuch crotchets in his pate,
　　And fuch ftrange notions,
She could not crofs the room without her mate
　　To watch her motions.
BINDOCCHIA was to be pity'd,
So watch'd, fo fcolded, fo ill fitted.

Confidering

Confidering cuckoldom's a fentence,
 That cannot be revers'd and null,
By commutation nor repentance,
 Nor by his Holinefs's Bull :


I cannot think he was to blame,
 So much as many folks pretend,
To fhut his doors, and to difclaim
 All intercourfe with ev'ry friend.


Thofe cuckolds, it can't be difputed,
 That either Heaven or earth can boaft,
Have been, and always are, cornuted
 By thofe in whom they truft the moft.


However, all were not deny'd ;
 He had a friend he valu'd next his life ;
A friend that he had often try'd ;
 One, by good luck, related to his wife.


He was admitted, night or day,
  To dine or fup,
  Or to ftep up,
If he was not inclin'd to ftay.
NICENO had an equal fhare
In the affections of this pair.

After

After much thought and perturbation,
   BINDOCCHIA grew to have less care,
For the continual defalcation
   In ANGRAVALLE's bills of fare---

Though you may think her patience strange,
   She thought, but not without some doubt,
The posture of affairs would change,
   That things would turn, and come about.

Two months were gone, which was a shame,
   Without receiving any news,
Though she had oft put in her claim,
   And often stickled for her dues;
The longer he was in arrear,
Her case and his grew still more queer.

In short, there was no end of waiting;
   Her Husband grew so great a debtor,
There was no way of calculating
   The chances of his growing better---

Now, Ladies, I desire to know,
   In such a situation,
Was it unnatural, or no,
   To cast her eyes on her Relation?

Observe,

Obferve, I faid to caft her eyes;
  With thofe 'twas natural to fpeak ;
To mingle alfo a few fighs,
  With a few rofes in each cheek :
Except a blufh, a figh, a foft regard,
All other forms of fpeech are barr'd.

Accordingly, within her lips
  She had a tongue in due fubjection ;
Not apt to wander, and make flips,
  Without her order and direction.

One day fhe went, upon leave granted,
  To fee her Coufin---pray, take notice, Sirs ?
A female that fhe often haunted,
  NICENO's Coufin too, as well as hers;
As ufual, attended by the Mute,
And by the Gardener, her fellow-brute---

PAULINA was her Coufin's name,
  A perfect Saint in her demeanour ;
Though fhe was fpotlefs in her fame,
  Never was any thing uncleaner :

She could impofe upon the Wife and Grave,
  And could, with TITUS, fafely fwear,
She never loft a day that fhe could fave,
  Nor fav'd a night that fhe could fpare.

                                        BINDOCCHIA

BINDOCCHIA told her Hufband's cafe,
　His former feats were not deny'd;
But then his fubfequent difgrace,
　By rhetorick was amplify'd.

By what means, or difcovery,
　Her Friend reply'd, can you be fure,
That he is paft recovery,
　That he is even paft your cure?

There's a diforder we call Fumbling,
　Amongft the men call'd Fighting fhy,
Teazing, tumbling, fqueezing, mumbling,
　Still worfe and worfe, the more they try.

Upon our fkill in this difeafe,
　All our whole happinefs depends;
All our importance, all our eafe,
　All our pow'r of obliging friends.

We muft, when call'd to their affiftance,
　Chearfully undergo the Law:
'Tis death to them to fhew refiftance,
　And worfe than death to laugh, or pfhaw.

With all their humours, all their fancies,
　In ev'ry form, in ev'ry fhape,
We muft comply; nay, make advances,
　To help them out of fuch a fcrape.

H

'Tis

'Tis by this fingle piece of fkill,
    That I command and rule,
    And make my headftrong mule
Submit entirely to my will.

BINDOCCHIA, indeed, I fear,
    That you, like many a Beauty,
Think that your goods ought to come clear
    Of ev'ry charge, and ev'ry duty :

And fo they will, my dear, by fmuggling ;
    But the foundation muft be laid,
By honeft induftry and ftruggling ;
    By credit in a lawful trade.
Have you with both your mind and might,
Endeavour'd to fet matters right ?

Cafting her eyes upon a crucifix,
    That hung within her coufin's bed ;
BINDOCCHIA faid, I have try'd all the tricks,
    That ever enter'd in a head.

I could as foon perfuade thofe thieves,
    To fteal away and leave their croffes ;
Or the fall'n tree with wither'd leaves,
    To rife, and to repair its loffes.
There never will be life within that lump,
'Till the dead rife at the laft trump.

PAULINA,

PAULINA, this is my decree,
  My Spouse muſt have a Coadjutor,
His Friend, all precedents agree,
  Should be preferr'd to ev'ry ſuitor.

I need not tell you whom I mean,
Nor aſk my Friend to go between :
He has had innuendo's many,
  But make NICENO underſtand,
That ſcruples, if he has any,
  Are juſt like letters wrote on ſand :

Or like the fears of truant boys,
  Which interrupt their briſk career,
And for a moment damp their joys,
  But the next moment diſappear :

Or like a boy in brief diſpute,
  Whether it is a ſin to pull
A pocket full of tempting fruit,
  Or rob an orchard that's quite full :
Nature decides, and doubt no longer hampers,
He fills his pockets, and he ſcampers.

    In fine,
  PAULINA reliſh'd her deſign,
Her Friend, by the ſame guard eſcorted,
  Return'd, to her old ſtation,
That night, PAULINA, 'tis reported,
  Finiſh'd her negotiation.

Her arguments had fo much weight,
NICENO gave up the debate.

BINDOCCHIA, put upon her mettle,
 Affembles and convenes,
Her powers, and all her wits, to fettle
 And find out ways and means:

She had not been an hour acquainted,
 With her Friend's motion and fuccefs,
'Till fhe was taken ill and fainted,
 And carry'd off, and forc'd t' undrefs.

Her mouth was drawn afide and purs'd,
 Her head turn'd like the flying chair,
 That children ride in at a fair;
Her ftomach fwell'd, and like to burft.

All night in bed fhe made a riot,
 Her Hufband thought fhe was poffefs'd,
She never had a moment's quiet,
 Nor he a fingle minute's reft.

Juft at the time that the cock crew,
Out of the bed BINDOCCHIA flew,
In the next chamber was a water clofet,
 Where fhe began to grunt and moan,
As if fhe was making a depofit,
 And was delivering a ftone.

Her

Her Hufband rofe and follow'd near,
  And if fhe had been off her guard,
She could have heard with half an ear,
  He puff'd, and fetch'd his breath fo hard,
By fmothering his cough he kept a wheezing,
Which for a lift'ner is as bad as fneezing.

Hearing him wheeze, fhe blew a gale,
  That feem'd to iffue from behind,
And made her Hufband turn his fail,
  And brufh away before the wind.

So well did fhe perform her part,
  Trumpeting with her mouth and hand;
He had no miftruft of any art,
  Or any dealings contraband.

At ev'ry foul report and crack,
  That fhe in agony let fly,
He mov'd, and flunk a little back,
  Like a judicious able fpy.

Scarce were they laid till he began to fnore,
BINDOCCHIA ftarted out of bed once more,
And foon fpoil'd ANGRAVALLE's fnoring;
  He thought it was a kettle-drum,
  For never any mortal bum,
Made fuch a rattling and roaring.

Again

Again he was upon his feet,
   Again she was all wind and griping;
Again he made a safe retreat,
   The inftant that he heard her wiping.

His jealous freaks were never fo kept under,
   But they would quickly fhoot and flow'r,.
To ev'ry one's aftonifhment and wonder,
   Like mufhrooms in a thunder fhow'r.

The moment he began to doze,
   It was in vain to think of fleeping;
She ftarted up, whipt on her cloaths,
   Ran off, and he came after creeping.

      'Till broad day-light,
There was no fign at all of ending,
   For fhe kept going all the night,
And he kept lift'ning and attending.
The female coufins, with much laughter,
Concerted all the fcenes hereafter.

Next day, the better to impofe,
   She kept her bed fatigu'd with purging,
And yet BINDOCCHIA often rofe,
   Her provocations were fo urging.

                                        The

The night was like the night before,
  Hurrying, trumpeting, difpatching:
The fame attendant at the door,
  For ever liftening and catching:
'Till he was weary'd out and fpent,
And quite convinc'd no harm was meant.

At three o'clock that very morning,
An hour convenient for horning,
NICENO, punctual to his call,
  In the next chamber was in waiting,
Convey'd thro' a window of the hall,
  Without much doubting and debating.

There was no fervant there to fear,
  Except the Mute, and none flept founder,
And fhe fo deaf, fhe could not hear
  Ev'n an eight and forty pounder.

The Gardener, by way of Groom,
  The only one watchful and able,
Laid at a diftance in a room,
    Over the ftable.

And now BINDOCCHIA went to reap,
  The fruits of all her labour,
Whilft ANGRAVALLE was afleep,
  She entertain'd his neighbour.

He

He was fo pleafant and engaging,
     She ftay'd with him three hours at leaft,
And tho' he wak'd coughing and raging,
     Her Hufband could not fpoil their feaft.

They went on joyoufly, for nothing caring,
     So keen is hunger;
Regarding him no more than a cheefe-paring,
     Or a Cheefemonger.

With her mouth fhe trumpeted and crack'd,
     And made a noife fo diabolick,
You would have fworn fhe had been rack'd,
     And torn to pieces with the cholick.

I may thank you for all I feel,
     Cry'd fhe to ANGRAVALLE, coughing,
If one was made of brafs or fteel,
     You would wear one out to nothing.

Three months with cold have I been dying,
By your pretty way of lying,
Such ufage is not to be borne,
     Toffing and kicking cloaths and fheets!
And never cover'd night nor morn!
     I could lie better in the ftreets!

Thus things being come to a conclufion,
     NICENO ftole away, fhe fhut up fhop,
Jump'd into bed without the leaft confufion,
     Scolded a while, and flept like any top.

END of the FIRST PART.

# ZACHARY'S TALE.

## PART II.

AT noon she rose, recover'd quite,
    Her colour and her eyes confefs'd,
They were fo radiant and bright,
    That nat'ral phyfick is the beft :
As ANGRAVALLE had foretold,
Natural phyfick carry'd off her cold.

What could not be foretold fo well,
    What he could only hope at moft,
That night fhe rais'd him, like a fpell
    Raifing the devil or a ghoft.

Her charms and efforts were fo great,
    His cure was compleated ;
Nay, 'twas fo thoroughly compleat,
    That all the proofs were twice repeated.

But this fhe knew fhe could not long rely on,
    Nor would it do by half ;
Unlefs a lamb will fatisfy a lion
    That can digeft a calf.

That half is far more than the whole,
    In former times, was HESIOD's thought ;
She was perfuaded from her foul,
    That half is only more than nought ;

And

And confequently lefs than half muft ftand,
Juft like a cypher, plac'd on the left hand.

    This fudden revolution
Caus'd, in her Hufband a revulfion,
    Which caus'd a refolution
To yield, and fellow its impulfion.
His country-houfe wanting repairing,
He thought to take a three days airing.

    Though he had vow'd a truft unfhaken
    For his BINDOCCHIA's late merits;
For all the trouble fhe had taken,
    To comfort him, and raife his fpirits;
Yet when he bade his wife adieu,
His jealoufy broke out anew.

    He left the Gardener inftructed;
    He was to watch and lie perdu,
To fee how matters were conducted,
    And to report upon a view:
And after this the Knight departed,
Sadly foreboding and faint-hearted.

His Lady knew, that time, like riches,
    Should be enjoy'd;
Which are but lumber in one's breeches,
    When unemploy'd:
Her greateft happinefs fhe ow'd
To time judicioufly beftow'd.

                  PAULINA

PAULINA was directed ſtrait
  The Coadjutor to ſecure;
He was that night to officiate
  In ANGRAVALLE's vacant cure:
For three whole nights, which is ſurprizing,
Was he employ'd in burying and baptizing.

After ſuch buſineſs and hurry,
  It ever was my confident belief,
That he was rather glad than ſorry,
  When ANGRAVALLE came to his relief;
Though the laſt night an accident fell out,
  That might alarm a man leſs ſtout.

Returning through the garden late,
  He ſpy'd, within the avery,
The Gardener lying in wait
  To perpetrate ſome knavery:

        Although betray'd,
He knew his Couſin's parts too well
        To be afraid
Of aught the Gardener could tell;
Nor ventur'd, in affairs ſo nice,
To interpoſe his own advice.

As to all ſalutary meaſures,
  He truſted to that native wit,
Abounding in inventive treaſures,
  And inexhauſtible as PITT---

In

In State Affairs, if not in Letters,
   NICENO may be an example,
When we give credit to our Betters,
   To make it generous and ample.
BINDOCCHIA thus, upon the brink of ruin,
Smil'd at the mischief that was brewing.


   She was peeping through her window lattice
      Just when she heard her Husband rap ;
         Not as a rat is,
     A rat that's peeping through a trap ;
         But as a cat is,
     A cat with a considering cap.


Whilst he was knocking at the gate,
   BINDOCCHIA slily descended ;
She knew the temper of her Mate,
   Enough to guess what he intended ;
Having, in cog, upon occasions,
   Assisted at his consultations.


The council-room was under-ground :
   Where he repair'd when he alighted,
The bill against his Spouse was found---
   And the poor soul, to be indicted ;
     A trial was decreed,
Proceedings settled and agreed.


                   The

The Court broke up, all parties to their tafk
  Till things fhould be reveal'd,
BINDOCCHIA iffu'd from an empty cafk,
  Where fhe had lain conceal'd.
Her Hufband took a turn or two
To fmooth the wrinkles on his brow---

Then fmiling, like a mind at eafe,
  He march'd up to his Lady's chamber,
And found BINDOCCHIA on her knees
  Before a crucifix of amber :
    A fituation,
That he beheld with indignation.

But he kept down his fwelling bile,
  Inform'd by fober reafon,
That his revenge, delay'd awhile,
  Would not be lefs in feafon ;
She neither mov'd her eye, nor her eye-brow,
'Till fhe had fung the Litany quite through.

Then rifing with a chearful air,
  So modeft, and fo unaffected,
That ANGRAVALLE well might ftare,
  When he confider'd and reflected.
However, with fome perturbation,
  He ftammer'd this Oration.

I muft

I muſt return---this afternoon,
 On bus'neſs, that I can't neglect;
To-morrow I will be here---ſoon;
 Sooner, perhaps,---than you expect.

I thought, if I did not appear,
 Knowing how great your love and care is,
That you would certainly, my Dear,
 Be full of fears and quandaries---
So I muſt inſtantly go back,
As ſoon as I have got a ſnack.

Whilſt this ſame ſnack was getting ready,
 PAULINA call'd upon her ſcholar,
A circumſtance that kept him ſteady---
 And help'd him to digeſt his choler.

His meal diſpatch'd, he ſet out in an amble,
 Full of his great and wiſe intentions,
BINDOCCHIA, in a ſhort preamble,
 Explain'd her doubts and apprehenſions,

Laid open all her plans and ſchemes,
 Her arguments and ſpeculations,
Which were ſo far from being dreams,
 PAULINA thought them revelations;
Her ſchemes, like Harlequinery,
Were all dumb ſhew and ſcenery;

        The

The whole, fo artfully invented,
  So free from all affected airs;
It muft fucceed, if reprefented,
  By any tolerable players.
PAULINA had a part affign'd,
In which her coufin knew fhe fhin'd.

They were refolv'd to try the event,
  And fet about it with good-will,
Knowing, before the night was fpent,
  They might be forc'd to fhew their fkill---
Which made PAULINA haften home,
To be prepar'd againft the time to come.

PAULINA told the Gard'ner in the entry,
  To mind her meffage, and take heed,
To leave his poft where he was fentry,
  And let his Lady know with fpeed,
That fhe had quite forgot to fay,
The meffage he was to convey.

That fhe had bus'nefs in the town,
  But fhe would fend the fringe and lace,
Drawings and patterns for the gown,
  By her own maid the Bolognoife.

BINDOCCHIA might keep her flattern,
  Keep her all night, if fhe requir'd,
'Till fhe had drawn and done the pattern,
  And the defigns that fhe defir'd.

'Tho' thefe were terms to him like Greek,
  Yet he deliver'd his commiffion,
And did, as well as he could fpeak,
  Deliver it with great precifion.

And now as foon as it was night,
  He lock'd the gates of the great court,
And introduc'd the jealous Knight,
  By a back way, or fally port.
Within the av'ry, in ambufcade,
His Lord and Mafter watch'd and pray'd.

Being firft inform'd how matters went,
That none had enter'd ever fince his going,
  Except a wench PAULINA fent,
That was above, drawing defigns for fewing,

A Bolognoife with fcarf and veil,
  Twanging through the nofe and fnuffing,
As if fhe had been from head to tail,
  Loaded with a Naples ftuffing.

The night was ftill, the moon was bright,
  When he, in an ill-fated hour,
Difcover'd plainly, by her light---
  NICENO paffing by his bow'r.
On which, with refolution,
He put his wrath in execution.

Our jealous Knight, in the firſt place,
  Summoned all his wife's relations;
As witneſſes of her diſgrace,
  And of his wrongs and patience,
Dragging along, with many others,
His Lady's father, and her brothers.


How did her brothers ſtorm, her father weep?
  When op'ning her room door, upon the bed,
They all beheld the Lovers faſt aſleep,
  Upon her boſom lay NICENO's head.


But when they ſaw the Lovers riſe,
How great their wonder, what muſt they ſuppoſe?
  They hardly could believe their eyes,
Seeing PAULINA in NICENO's cloaths---
And here the injur'd wife began to hector,
  Reading the following lecture.


His jealous fits were ev'ry hour,
  Nay, ev'ry minute, growing ſtronger,
'Till he had put it paſt my pow'r,
  To bear his folly any longer.


Having obſerv'd the jealous fool
  Following me when I was ſick,
Every time I went to ſtool,
  I own it touch'd me to the quick.


K

PAULINA's goodhefs and devotion,
   Was fhock'd at my determination,
Infifting it was a rafh notion,
   Altho' fhe own'd the provocation ;
Advifing me to club our wits,
To try to cure my Hufband's fits.


Whilft ANGRAVALLE was away,
   Indeed, I blufh whilft I am fpeaking,
I fpy'd the Gard'ner, where he lay,
   Watching like a thief, and fneaking.


So having found the thing I fought,
   A key that turn'd the garden door lock,
I was tranfported with the thought,
   Of punifhing my ftupid block.


PAULINA, as fhe had often done,
Borrow'd her coufin's cloaths, and in the garden;
   In order to compleat our fun,
Appear'd before the Gardener, my warden.


My fpoufe, we did not doubt the leaft,
   Would be inform'd as we defir'd,
We knew that the fufpicious beaft,
   With rage and vengeance would be fir'd.

His second going was to deceive,
  It happen'd juſt as we ſuppos'd,
And now I humbly conceive,
  He is ſufficiently expos'd---
    This is the hiſtory,
    Of all this myſtery:
And now I beg, his temper ſuch is,
To be deliver'd from his clutches.


Her Huſband, touch'd with true compunction,
  Acknowledg'd his tranſgreſſions,
She ſpoke with ſo much force and unction,
  He promis'd before all the ſeſſions,
    If ſhe would pardon what was paſt,
    That this offence ſhould be the laſt.


And as a proof that his deſigns were good,
  The Gard'ner ſhould be diſcarded;
She ſhould chuſe ſervants, and go where ſhe would
    Unguarded.


BINDOCCHIA conſented,
  And never afterwards repented.
  PAULINA to her maid retir'd,
Which maid was not according to the letter,
  But in this faſhion was attir'd,
On purpoſe to conceal NICENO better.

So

So well he acted, I'll engage,
That this NICENO might have play'd
On any theatre or ftage,
The fnuffling Bolognia maid.
PAULINA drefs'd herfelf before fhe went,
Her maid had brought her cloaths for that intent.

People that I fufpect for fcoffers,
Pretend that whilft PAULINA was undreffing,
NICENO made her handfome offers,
Which fhe could not refufe, he was fo preffing.
They were together, 'tis confefs'd,
Two hours before fhe could get drefs'd.

However 'twas is undecided,
But as to him he was compleat,
In every circumftance provided,
And fit to ferve a pious cheat,
But, to be able to ferve two,
Is more than either you or I can do.

THE

# THE

# PRIVY-COUNSELLOR'S

### AND THE

# STUDENT of LAW'S TALE.

## A MANUSCRIPT

## Found at CRAZY-CASTLE.

Suppofed to be wrote about the Time of HENRY VIII.

# PROLOGUE

## TO THE

## PRIVY-COUNSELLOR'S

### AND THE

## STUDENT of LAW's TALE.

ONCE on a time, how many years ago,
  As I could nivir learn, you cannot know,
    A Member of the Parliment,
  And a Law-ftudent, his relation,
    Rode out of town with no intent,
  Unlefs it was for recreation.
Full fixty is the Member, and hath feen
Many a famous King, and comely Queen
    In yvery reign, in yvery age,
  He florifh'd in profperitie:
    In the beginning was a Page,
    Now Privy-Counfellor is he.
His perfonage is grave and full of ftate,
Yielding him weight and vantage in debate;
But with a boon-companion gay and free;
  No ceremony, no myfterious airs;
Juft as a Privy-Counfellour fhould be,
  If he had been a Page of the Back-ftairs.
The Student's Father is in perfect health,
Thank God, and waxes daily ftrong in wealth;

Wants

Wants not his fon to get a heap,
  But juft enough of Law,
To guard his own Eftate, and keep
  The Neighbourhood in awe ;
And I dare venture to maintain,
Herein his Father's hopes fhall not be vain.
Allbeit, he doth not attend the Courts,
And redith none but GEOFFERY's Reports ;
Yet PLOWDEN lying ever on the table,
    Opin and fpread,
  He is counted full as able,
    As if he had him in his head.
So, as I fignify'd before, thefe two
Ride out of town, having nought elfe to do.
Six miles from town, this Member hath a box.
    For contemplation good ;
Where he retires, as thoughtful as an ox
    Chewing his cud.
  He creeps into his box of ftone,
    Sometimes for pleafure, oftener for whim ;
  Or when he is tir'd of every one,
    Or every one is tir'd of him.
It is call'd a Box, and there's a reafon why,
Becaufe therein a man lies himfelf by---
Within a box, if you your cloaths conceal,
  The fafhion and the worms confpire,
To make a fuit, that was genteel,
  Fit only for the Sheriff of a fhire ;
    But good enough for you,
If in your box you lie too long perdu.

When

When you come out again, 'twill be too late;
You and your coat will both be out of date---
Here then they light, and now fuppofe them dining;
Suppofe them alfo grumbling and repining ;.
The bacon's fufty, and the fowls are tough;
The mutton over-done, the fifh not done enough ;
The cloth is drawn, the wine before them fet ;
Wine, like themfelves, entirely on the fret :
Muttering their prayers, exchanging looks afkew,
Juft like two rival beauties in a pew.
　　What might have happen'd no one can decide,
　　　　Had not, by fortune or defign,
　　　The Butler in the cellar fpy'd
　　　A hoard of admirable wine :
Bounce goes the cork ; fparkles the glafs ;
Coufin, here's to your favourite lafs :
　　　And here their purgatory ends ;
　　　　　For after this
　　　They enter into perfect blifs,
　　　Drinking like perfect friends :
Drinking, becaufe drinking promoteth joaking ;
Joaking without infulting or provoking.
　　The evening finifhes with equal glory,
　　　The worthy Counfellor propofing
　　　　　To make a clofing,
　　By telling each a merry ftory.
I have one fram'd, fays he, in GEOFFRY's phrafe ;
GEOFFRY's the Courtier's language of thofe days.
　　The Student likes the motion well ;
Says he, I'll anfwer you with one quite new---.
　　My tale in courtly fpeech I cannot tell ;
But I can tell a merry tale, and true.

THE

# PRIVY-COUNSELLOR'S TALE.

## TALE V.

REIGNID in Yorkſhire one of mity fame,
Clepid King GRIG, as Kronikels proclaim;
Thilk Prince delighted ay in mirth and ſport,
Japis and jollitries of yvery ſort;
And now when pepil lough, and rage, and play,
Folk name them merry Grigs until this day---
This King, I undirſtond, hath venimid his blud,
Whereby he hath loſt his corage and his rud;
Sore ſhent is he by Cupid and his mother,
And woe-begone far more than any other---
The Kingis mother dere, Queen WHITY hight,
Becauſe her heer, allſo her ſkin is white,
Is Queen of Cortefy, and Beautis Pride,
Gentil and modeſt as a maidin bride.
She ſends to Potikers and Leeches grave,
Prays them to ſpare his life, and membris ſave;
Ne drogue ne inſtroment mote him avail;
His joints are loſen'd, and his cheekis pale;
And he that erſt would ſing, and laugh, and jeer,
Hath not he ſmilid once in haf a year.
    There is à Conjorer, a ſottil Wight;
This Conjorer the Queen conſults by night.

Clepid, called. Thilk, this fame. Japis, jeſts. Rage, frolick. Venimid
his blud, tainted. Corage and his rud, his ſtrength, his ſpirits, and complexion.
Shent, hurt. Hight, called. Heer, hair. Leeches, phyſicians. Erſt, formerly. Haf, half. Sottil wight, a cunning fellow.

L

The Neekromanzir, according to his guife,
Cafteth his figures, poreth on the fkies,
And redith how to cure the Kingis woe;
His Grace until an heling-well fhall go,
And bath his lims for fivin nights therein;
And fivin maidins, ftrippid to the fkin,
Shall *frote* his body, 'till one, by her devife
And cunning touching, hele him in a trice.

    Both King and Queen, you may be very fure,
Are in great hafte to fet about the cure.
Now is fhe fetten forth in brave array,
And with the *fely* King upon her way;
*Yccompany'd* with Minftrels and *Japers*,
Jugglirs and Morrice-dancers, cutting capers;
One time that thing which Minifters delite,
Shall, in another feafon, breed difpite;
For when the King is fad, it is ungracious thing
If *everich-one* is merrier than the King.
In this fort journeying, they come at laft
Unto the well, wherein the King him caft;
His body chafid is, with fpecial care,
By fivin naked damfills paffing fair.

    The King hath view'd them well in every *piece*,
Withouten fplint, or malanders, or greafe;
Hard are their breaftis, fkin as fmothe as glafs;
Plomp be their bottoks, and as tight as brafs;
Smale are their feet; each feature, every limb,
Lies in the faireft form, and fweeteft trim---

*Frote*, rub.   *Sely*, fick.   *Yccompany'd*, accompany'd.   *Japers*, Jefters.
*Everich*, every   *Piece*, part.

                                   The

The Queen examinid hath craftily
For Maidins of the beſt virginity;
None of theſe fivin hath ſpilt her maidins-hede,
As in theſe days moch reſon was to drede.
Handlid and chaſid with *ſick daintyneſs,*
*Wexid* the King to gather *luſtyneſs;*
And *notabul* it is to *everich* eye,
How he is rais'd and cheriſhed thereby.
The fivinth day they all are out of pain;
Symptome of helth appeärid very plain;
Whereat the Queen rejoices as is need,
Honoring the Maidin who hath done the deid;
And yet when he returnid hath to Court,
The King *mote* not be pleas'd in any ſort;
And all that Lords and Ladys can invent,
Shall but encreaſe the Kingis diſcontent;
Wherfor the dutyfull Queen hieth her,
And counſelleth again the Conjorer.

He ſpieth, in his ſecret *Boke of Magie,*
How the ſame Maidins *mote him rectifie;*
And yvery buxom Maid ſhall ſpeke a tale,
And yvery Maid to make him lough affail;
And ſhe that makes him lough ſhall thence be led,
And have the Kingis company in bed;
In bed, or any other pleaſant place,
Wherever it ſhall pleaſe the Kingis Grace.

---

*Sik,* ſuch. *Daintyneſs,* elegance. *Luſtyneſs,* ſtrength, health, &c. *Nota-bul,* plain. *Everich,* every. *Mote,* might. *Boke of Magie,* Conjuring book. *Mate,* might. *Rectifie,* ſet him to rights.

And lo the Queen thefe joyful tidings bears
To Chappil, where the Maidins are at prayers---
•Away the Maidins hurry them from Matins,
Apparrelling themfelves in filks and fattins;
And all the fivin Damzils, out of hand,
Are fet before the King at his command---
He doth ordain each Maid to fpeke by lot;
Allfo, becaufe ne word fhall be forgot,
A Scribe is there to notice all they fay---
And now fix Maids have talk'd for haf a day;
And yet, for all the talking they can make,
They fcarce can keep the Kingis Grace awake.
Then came the fivinth Maidin in degree,
But cannot fpeke her tale for modefty.

   My tale, faies fhe, I wold begin, but fear
A word unfeemly to a modeft ear;
My tale without this word cannot be told,
And to deliver it I am not bold---
What means the Maidin, quoth the King *in ire*,
You may *gloze* any word if you *enquire* ?
I am no *Clerk*, faies fhe, her Grace well knows,
Pleafith you, Sir, may teach me how to *gloze*;
Bot I will trie to do the beft I may,
That you may better frame what I would fay---
Of all God's creatures its the choiceft fare,
Yet he that has the leaft, has the beft fhare.
I fhall not graunt your prayer, the King reply'd,
Riddils are derk; and Paraphrafe is wide:

   *In ire*, in a paffion. *Enquire*, ftudy. *Clerk*, fcholar. *Gloze*, to wrap up
ænigmatically.

                                           Bot

Bot well I know the Latin and the Dutch,
Of Fraunce and Tofcany I have a touch:
Now, any of thefe tongues, if you're enclin'd,
Fair Maid, may feem to fhape what you would find.
Dutch, quoth the Queen, my fon, the maid demands,
It is a tongue no Chriftian undirftands.
Well, quoth the King, fair Maid, this dredefull name,
That werkith in you fo much ftrife and fhame,
Pronounce they Fotz throughout all Germany;
Now you may fpeke your ftory *hardily*. ---

Sir, quoth the buxom Maid, upon a time,
A jolly Knight there was in all his prime,
*Soot* were his eyes, and manly was his face,
Lufty his limbs, his body in good cafe;
A piercing and a pleafant wit withall,
Ne vice had he, but that *his means* were fmall:
Here the King turning, doth the Scribe befeech,
To lofe no word, nor fentence of her fpeech.

Upon a *joyful tide*, the King of Kent
Proclamid hath, a noble turnament,
There yvery Knight enforced is to be;
Unlefs he will be *held of villanie*;
Our Knight, Sir AMADOR the debonaire,
Mote thither with his Squire and fteed repair:
And having traveled five days *anend*,
The Knight and Squire unto a meadow *wend*,
Ynamilid with pinks and cowflips gay,
Thro' which a rivir glides as bright as fummir-day,

*Hardily*, boldly. *Soot*, fweet. *Means*, Fortune, Eftate. *Joyfull Tide*, Time of Feftivity. *Held of Villanie*, degraded and reduc'd to the condition of a Vaffal. *Anend*, ftrait forwards. *Wend*, arriv'd.

Upon

Upon the banks grows many a beachin tree,
And many a fpreding oak moft fair to fee;
There they efpied in the criftal lake,
Three nakid damzills of an hevenly make;
Their *wimples* and their gowns of *broudid* filk,
Ywrought with gold, their fmokkis white as milk,
And all their coftly garments were difplay'd
Undir an aged oak's ynticing fhade.

  Behold the Knightis color changeth hue,
At fight fo unexpected and .fo new;
Not that Acteon's hap *ydraddid* he,
Worried belike for *fik* audacity.
The Knight he blofh'd, becaufe he *thote* within,
Such nakidnefs fhall make a faint to fin.---
Gazeth Sir AMADOR with all his mite,
Tafteth thereof the 'Squire but brief delite,
For being more ynclined unto prey,
Stealid their fmokkis and their robes away.
The Maidens noted the unworthy Swain,
And calling to the Knight, declare their pain;
Soon the ynragid Knight arrefts the Squire,
And turnith to the Maids with their attire,
Making excufes, he could do no lefs,
For his intrufion on their nakidnefs,
And with profound refpect and reverence,
Saluting each by turns he bears him hence.

  He is hardly gone, before they all agree,
They fhould have done the Knight fome cortefy;

---

*Wimples,* . Neck-kerchief.   *Eroudid,* embroider'd.   *Ydraddid,* fear'd.
*Thote,* thought.   *Sik,* the like.

And

And call him back; the eldeſt Suſter ſpoke,
Sir, we be Fairys living by this *broke*,
And *ſikirly* unfit it is for us,
That have ſuch power, to be diſcourteous;
Wherfore ſome tokins at our hands receive,
And for myſelf, this tokin will I leave,
Wymen to pleaſure you ſhall ever ſtrive
In any land, ſo long as you're alive,
And you ſhall nivir fail in wymen's pleaſure,
And when you pleaſe, ſhall pleaſe them without meaſure.

   The ſecond Fairy ſaith, Sir Knight, my tokin
Is of a nature wondros to be ſpokin---
And now the Damzill's tale cannot proceed;
Her face, as any burning coal, is rede.
Quoth then, the King divining ſottely,
The word you ſeek, is Fotz aſſuredly:
True, ſaies the Maid; and ſo the Fairy ſaith,
That whoſoever Fotz he queſtioneth,
Shall make an anſwer, or if none ſhe gives,
The Fotz ſhall fare the worſe for't whilſt ſhe lives.

   My Suſter, quoth the third, under correction,
Your tokin's good, but lacketh of perfection,
The Fotz may be, by accidental cauſe,
So buſy that ſhe cannot move her jaws;
Whenever this doth happen, I intend
Her next door neighbour anſwer for her friend---
The King no longer can refrain from laughter,
Alſo the Queen herſelf him follows after.
I will reward you well for this anon;
Mean time, quoth he, my pritty Maid, go on.

      *Broke*, brook,  *Sikirly*, certainly.

The

The Knight *ne yvir* having feen a *fay*,
Thinketh they *japen* him in that they fay---
He overtakes the Squire, and on they ride,
Difcourfing on the Fairys, fide by fide;
Happened a *Freer* of a neighboring abbey,
Rideth abroad in gallant pomp that day,
Mounted he is upon a dapple mare,
And loketh altogether void of care,
Rofy his cheeks, a twinkling hazle eye,
He feemid Patriarke of Venerie;
Or, Pontif of renowned *Baal-Peor*,
Certes you fhall not oft meet fuch a Freer,

*Ne yvir*, never. *Fay*, Fairy. *Japen*, banter. *Freer*, Friar.

*Baal-Peor*, or *Baal-Phegor*, from whence, perhaps, *Pego*, and the adjunct Βαλλοκ, whofe priefts are opprobrioufly called Βαλλοκς, or *Followers of Baal-Peor*; who, according to Dr. Middleton, was a god of the Moabites, the fame with *Priapus*. (See *Germana quædam monumenta*, by Dr. Conyers Middleton, S. T. P. in Quarto, page 65, with two monuments elegantly engraved of Βαλλοκ-ωιγω.) The Doctor fays, from the authority of the Fathers, that he was the hobby-horfe of the women of Ifrael, page 69.—That the new-married women had an *Idolum Tentiginis*, which our language is incapable of rendering; and, that they not only took great delight in getting aftride of this idol, but they were enjoined to do fo as a religious ceremony. The Doctor has given a defcription of one of thefe idols, which he has had the good fortune to fee at Rome. As our Ladies are not under any obligation to practife all the ceremonies of the Ladies of Ifrael, I am lefs concerned at my want of erudition to explain to them fufficiently the meaning of feveral of the Doctor's terms.

The idol's head is like the head of a cock, but inftead of a beak, is a ftupendous *Fafcinum*: upon the bafe is infcribed, ΣΩΤΗΡ ΚΟΣΜΟΥ, *the Saviour of the World.*

I cannot believe (however refpectable the authority) that the children of the Roman nobility wore the *Fafcinum* about their necks: I do not mean that it is an unbecoming ornament; one may be eafily convinced of the contrary, by cafting an eye upon the two belonging to the Doctor and his friend Dr. Warren, with which, as I faid before, he has obliged the Publick, in his Genuine Antiquities; but, confidering the ingenuity of the Romans, why might not their *Fafcinum* be the fame, and for the fame purpofe, as that of the Chinefe?—If the Doctor had feen thofe of Mrs. Chenivix, he certainly would have been of another opinion. But, what is the moft remarkable of all, is, that in the Chinefe language Διλω fignifies *a charm*. A convincing argument of the weaknefs of an hypothefis, fupported only by the etymology of words.

The

The Knight accofteth him, noteth the beaft,
The dapple mare that bears the ftately prieft;
Fotz, faies the Knight, I queftion thee to fay,
Whither thy mafter hieth him this way?
Finding fhe needs muft anfwer him par force,
Diftinctly anfwers Fotz, tho' fomewhat hoarfe,
What you require I will deliver brief,
My mafter is *avowterer* and thief;
He hath robb'd the facrefty of churches plate,
And to his *lemman* beareth it in ftate.---
The Prieft, aftony'd fuch a voice to find,
Believeth Sathanas is there behind;
Defcendeth from the mare, voweth repentaunce,
Leaving the Knight talking with new acquaintance;
The Prieft is lame, and no great haft can make;
He waddles like a duck eftir a drake.

Fotz, quoth the Knight, pray tell me as we go,
What is it makes the Freer waddil fo?

Sir, quoth the Fotz, about a year agon,
Our Abbot and my Mafter, Freer JOHN,
Difcourfing, riding round the Abbot's Perk,
Of leachery and prankis in the derk;
The Abbot foftly *rounith* brother JOHN,
All fauncies have I *proven* everich one,
Whereby a man may find the greateft joy,
The pleafanteft his talent to employ---
Yet thereto, though I oft have been inclin'd,
Have not I yvir practic'd *out of kind.*

*Avowterer,* adulterer. *Lemman,* Miftrefs. *Rounith,* whifpers. *Proven,*
tried. *Out of kind,* unnaturally.

Nor I, fays Freer JOHN, I do declare ;
Trie we then, fays the Abbot, with the mare :
But reafon giveth property the place,
Wherefor thyfelf fhalt have the firft embrace.
Freer confents, and, for his evil deeds,
Ungirds the cords whereon he ftrings the beads ;
Bindeth therewith nine hinder leggis twain,
Holdeth me faft the Abbot by the rein ;
And letting go his fteed, he praunceth by,
And with a kick lamid the Freer's thigh ;
Elfe had I been, upon my corp'ral oath,
Ravyfhed by a Freer and Abbot both.

   Now forward Knight and ftrange companion trots,
Laughing the Knight, and communing with Fotz ;
Upon a hill not far they do defcry
A caffil fair, with *towris* broad and high ;
Shaped their courfe unto the caffil ftrait ;
Opin'd the Porter hath the caffil-gate.
The Senefchal hath led the Squire and Knight
Through goodly chambris curiofly *bedight,*
Unto an hall hung round with tapeftry,
Of PHAROH's hoft, *drenchid* in the Rede Sea,
There at their fupper fit the Gouvernante,
Or Lady of the Caffil, and her Ant ;
This Lady is a Wedo frefh and young
And frolikfome, and hath a merry tong----
And looks fo kind, and fings fuch lovefome ftrains,
No marvel that her Lord hath *braft* his reins.

*Towris,* towers. *Drenchid,* drowned. *Tong,* tongue. *Braft,* broke.

Welcome,

Welcome, Sir Knight, faies fhe, unto my board,
I have not feen a Nobler fince my Lord.
The Knight and 'Squire fit them down to eat,
The board is cover'd with all kind of meat;
Rich wines the pages pour in chriftal glafs,
And many a choice conceit and laugh doth pafs.
The hour is late; tarrieth the Aunt for fpite,
Rifeth the Lady---wifheth a good night.
The Knight in bed, *ay* thinketh on his hoft,
Sleep hath he none, for wantonnefs of ghoft.
This bounteous Wedo gives her maids a call,
Chufing the beft, and faireft of them all;
Biddeth her go unto the Knight, and fay,
She comes to folace him 'till it is day.
And that her Lady bids her fay in bed,
How much fhe wifhes fhe was in her ftead:
Bot may not have the opportunity,
Becaufe, for fpite, the Aunt with her doth lie.
The maidin flies; her heart with gladnefs beats,
Strippith, and creepith in between the fheets.
Turnith the Knight unto the maidin gent,
And both do pafs the time with moch content---
And aftir they have ragid to the full,
Strokid the Knight, and givith Fotz a pull,
And faieth, little Fotz, tellith me true,
Be you aggriev'd with that I have done at you---
As I am a Chriftian, Fotz, replied fhe,
I nivir pafs'd a night with fo much glee---

*Ay*, always.

Up fterts the Maidin, runnith in difmay,
Into the room next that her Lady lay,
And finds her Lady up, and fitting there,
Mufing and pond'ring in an elbow-chair.
YonKnight, quoth fhe's a witch, or fomething badder,
He conjur'd hath the Devil in my bladder;
After he did me twenty times and more,
Oftner than ever I was done before;
He pulleth Fotz, and of its own accord,
Spekid the mouth that nivir utters word---
Child, quoth the Lady, fet your mind at eafe,
Moft of us all have have had the like difeafe,
Working anights at foch a grievous rate,
Lozens the Fotz's tongue, and makes it prate;
The Lady thinks to humour her is beft,
She deems her head is light for want of reft---
Yes, faies the Maid, they have tongis without doubt,
I have feen Fotzes tongis hanging out.
Go, get to reft, replies the Lady bright,
A little fleep will fet your matters right.
The Maidin goes, the Lady at the dore
Harkneth, and ftealeth to Sir AMADORE;
Sir Knight, quoth fhe, it is not very civil,
To give my Maidin's Fotz unto the Devil:
Fotz is no chamber for fo mean a groom,
He might have been content with a worfe room.
I ufe no fiend, quoth he, but have a fkill,
To make what Fotz I pleafe, talk when I will---
Talk, faies the Lady, I engage this ring,
You neither make it talk, whyffel, nor fing---

Out

Out flew the Knight, moft terribly array'd;
At fight whereof the Dame was nought afraid---
Upon the bed the Lady hath he pitch'd,
And there fhe lay, as if fhe was bewitch'd:
And after many pleafaunt fauncies there,
Breethed the Knight awhile, to take the air;
And whifpering the Fotz, holding his nofe,
Biddith my Lady Fotz tell all fhe knows.
Gapid the Fotz, and gabbill'd far and wide,
Telling foch things, the Wedo fwore fhe lied.
I yield, faies fhe---you are a fkilful youth;
I yield, if you will ftop that lyar's mouth---
'Tis mighty well, faies he, we foon fhall trie,
Whether my Lady Fotz has learnt to lie---
And thrufting into Fotz's mouth a gag,
Her next door neighbour's tong began to wag.
Saies fhe, in a crack'd voice, like one you feign,
All that Fotz fayth I am ready to maintain.
Enough, the Lady faith, Sir Knight, have done,
Here, take the ring, I own 'tis fairly won;
And fince you are a Knight of fo great power,
Freely I offer both myfelf and dower;
And certes one was made for t'other's fake---
For you can give no more than I can take.
    The fabul's finifhed, the King is *hele*,
The Damzill is contented yvery deal;
And GRIG had fons, and they had many heirs,
And they were all like GRIG, all free from cares,
Their hearts would nivir fink no more than cork,
And tho' no Kings, they ftill are Dukes of York.
        *Hele*, whole recovered.

# The STUDENT of LAW's TALE;

O R,

# The CURE for SYMPATHY.

## TALE VI.

SIGN of the Lamb, near Ludgate, you may find
    The sign is emblem of the owner's mind,
EMANUEL COOPER dwelleth in that place,
A Mercer, with an yvir-smiling face,
Speking so soft, and pityfull, and meek,
It seems he rather bleateth than doth speke;
All pepil that do pass he humbly greets,
Nay, when the wanton stops him in the streets,
Tho' he doth most abhor the harlot's waies;
That she will let him go, he sofily praies;
Altho' she holds him fast he will not swear,
But, yvir-smiling, doth intreat her fair---
He hath heard his Onkil say, there is ne vice
He mote eschew like Harlotry and Dice;
Harlots make men unfit to get an heir,
And Dice consume all that the Harlots spare.
This Onkil is a Scriv'nir in the Strond,
Is rich, and lendeth money upon lond,
A batchellor, and old, and dredeful sly,
And trustith not to possibillity:
For he will see EMANUEL have a son,
Before he builds the house at Edmonton,

- With golden letters wrote upon the wall,
Advising folk to name it Cooper-hall.
    The way EMANUEL toke to get a wife,
Is subject of this Tale, and best of all his life.
EMANUEL hath near served out his years,
Having ne vice at all the Onkil fears,
Ne caufe the Onkil hath to be afraid,
Vice hath he none but craftynefs of trade.
And now above a month his maftir's gone
To drink the rede cow's milk at Yflington,
And yvery day they loke for him to die
Of a Confomption and the Lipprofie,
And for that he doth truft EMANUEL,
He leaveth him alone to buy and fell.
His Dame was brought up high, and knows not trade,
To an Earl's Countefs was fhe waiting-maid,
Rofys for rings contrives, and rhimes indites,
And can difcourfe, either with Squires or Knights
Having quaint terms, and phrafes to propound,
Which thofe that dwell by Poul's cannot expound,
But fhe hath long been very fick, and vows,
How fhe hath got the ficknefs of her Spoufe,
Her Hufband's kindred alfo do proclaim,
How he hath got the ficknefs of the Dame;
That fhe hath fecret drogues, and but pretends
To ufe the drogues her Hufband's Doctor fends:
And fo by following another courfe,
She is grown better, and the Hufband worfe.
His Doctor fays, that fhe is whole and pure,
And doubteth not that he hath done the cure:

Her

Her Spoufe will not be cur'd, the Doctor fees,
Becaufe of complication of difeafe.
Doctor and ISABELL maintain it ftill
That ISABELL was fmit by RICHARD's ill;
RICHARD rejoices fhe hath gained helth,
Maketh his will, and leaveth her his welth.

ISABELL's eye hath notic'd many a time,
EMANUEL COOPER entering in his prime,
And hath delighted, many a time, to fee,
Soch perfect maiden-like fimplicitie.
One evening in her chamber fhe will fup,
And bids the Maid to call EMANUEL up;
Blofhing, and hanging down his heade, he comes,
Sitting him down, and loking at his thumbs---
Upon the bed by her fhe makes him fit,
And helpeth him to yvery dainty bit;
Come, faies the Dame, filling a cup quite up,
Take off this wine, I will not bate a fup:
Unto my Maftir's helth, quoth he, and drinks it dry;
Lord take his foul, faies fhe, and falls to cry,
Name him no more, for it will break my heart,
The Doctor faies, that he fhall foon depart,
And alfo faies, that when my Spoufe is flain,
I fhall not after him long time remain,
By fympathy his malady I have,
And fympathy fhall join us in the grave:
The remedy for fympathy is fure,
But it is one I nivir will endure:

Quoth then EMANUEL, weeping as he fpoke,
Your cafe would pierce a heart, if it was oak,
Bot if you flay the life that you may fpare,
It is a fin as dedely as defpair.
You fpeke devout, quoth fhe, but Hea'v'ns a friend
To all that mean no ill, when they offend.
Quoth he, that is but *fotelty*, I fear,
For where the law is plain, the fault is clear;
Is it not written, that you fhall not kill?
Therefor the crime is both in deed and will:
I do confefs, quoth fhe, ftroaking her ring,
Deep is the judgment of your reafoning---
Befides, faies he, my Maftir may mend yet;
With that at once fhe falls into a fit,
Catches EMANUEL by the hand, and faies,
For mercy's fake, EMANUEL, cut my ftaies.
EMANUEL takes a knife and cuts the ftring,
And ISABELL about his waift doth cling:
Feel but my heart, faies fhe, how it doth beat,
Put in your hand, EMANUEL, farther, fweet.
In footh, quoth he, you are in piteous hap,
The maid had beft come up:---I'll give a rap.
No, no, quoth fhe, I thank you for your love,
Sit down upon the bed, you fhall not move;
Pity for me, hath wrought in you diftrefs,
Another cup will cure your hevynefs.
The wine, to make it richer cordial,
Mingled the Dame, Cantharides withall;
EMANUEL drinks it up, the wine is choice,
Wipeth his mouth, and cleareth up his voice:

*Sotelty,* Subtilty.

N

Madam,

Madam, quoth he, if Heaven doth intend,
To take away my Maſtir, and my friend,
The byſneſs of the ſhop I'le undertake,
Both for your own, and for my Maſtir's ſake.
In that I am contented well, quoth ſhe,
Could I but take the Cure for Sympathy:
It is a filthy Cure---EMANUEL, mark;
You may ſuppoſe yourſelf to be the ſpark:
Take a young ſpark, it ſays, and let him be,
A maid and modeſt, not paſt twenty-three:---
From twenty-three ſhall he begin to count,
And do the deed, 'till he to thirty mount;
And he muſt ſecret ſwear; and alſo both
Shall bind their member, with a fearfull oath
That neither. he nor ſhe ſhall find delite,
But do the act; as if it was for ſpite.
Quoth then EMANUEL, ſtiff as any ſtake,
For now the wine hath made him quite awake,
As to the maiden-term am not afraid;
As Bleſſid MARY, am I very maid:
I am but three and twenty yeſterday;
But for the oath I know not what to ſay;
I am content myſelf it ſo ſhould be,
If that the members alſo will agree.
That's in your power, ſaies ſhe, there is no doubt,
If you'll not think of what you are about;
You muſt continue, when you are occupy'd,
To think of any other thing beſide.
For inſtance; when you are arrived there,
Keep thinking of a rabbit or a hare.---

And we need never feel, nor know no more
Than doth the ſhuttle-cock and battle-dore ;
Without more words, this treaty ſhall have force,
And all the reſt are only forms of courſe.
Leave we the parties interchangeably,
To take the ſolemn oath, and ratify.
They both went on, thinking and nothing ſaying,
'Till the laſt payment of the ſum was paying;
And then EMANUEL cried out, I find
I cannot keep the hare within my mind;
When once you fall a ſpinning like a top,
Rabbit and hare out of my mind do hop---
Go on, you fool, ſaies ſhe, What makes you ſtop.
The ſum is paid, yet ſtill in bed they lay;
Her Sympathy is not quite ſweat away :
Up ſtairs the maiden comes, raps at the dore,
Shouting, my Maſtir's dede for yvirmore;
His man from Yſlington, doth ſay, below,
That he went off as any child ſhall go.
Shout not, the Dame replies, I underſtand,
Holding EMANUEL's handle in her hand.
Run to the Undertaker of our ſtreet;
I fear me RICHARD will not long keep ſweet :
I go, quoth ſhe, EMANUEL this day,
Too far for health to loſe it in the way :
And as it needs muſt be provoking pain
To run this race of penitence again,
And as---your three and twentieth year is out,
It is but ſafe to take another bout :
If this had been but a pretence or trick,
She mote have pleaded falſe Arithmetick;         But

But, as fhe fairly own'd the whole receipt,
It's evident fhe had no defign to cheat;
And fo EMANUEL, after fome paufe,
Mended the bill, and put in a new claufe---
I will not paint the difmal funeral;
The Wedo's lamentations tragical;
Whofo delighteth to depicture woe,
Richly deferveth wretchednefs allfo :
Yet can I not defcribe, without a figh,
The penalties that wait on perjury.
EMANUEL is forefworn; it is his doom
To languifh with one foot within the tomb :
For three whole moons in raging pain he lay---
The fourth the perjur'd limb is fnatch'd away---
Heaven is appeas'd at laft, EMANUEL found,
And for fo fmall a lofs glad to compound.
What great Philofophers obferve is true,
Allthough a Member will not grow anew;
Yet, notwithftanding this, the member brother
Fares better for the abfence of the other;
For, when they go together in a pair,
The next furviving brother is the heir;
But if they're fingle, and the right not plain,
The benefit devolves upon the brain;
And thus EMANUEL, having need of it,
Receives a pritty legacy in wit:
He gives the Potiker and Surgeon fee
To keep the lofs of Member fecrecy.
    No longer to the Chainge EMANUEL reforts,
He is allwaies at the Stews and Inns of Courts;

He drinks and beats the Watch, lies out anights,
Living with Lawyers Clerks and wicked Wights,---
In greateft grief is interval of eafe ;
One day the Wedoe feizeth one of thefe,
Calleth EMANUEL, fheweth plain the cafe,
How, from the lewdnefs of his laft embrace,
It happens that fhe is not healid quite---
Trie to be more compos'd, faies fhe to-night.
Compos'd, EMANUEL faith ! it cannot be ;
With you I needs muft feel felicitie.
To do an act like this from generous fenfe,
Without defire, is true benevolence : .
Benevolence belongs to marry'd life ;
'Tis what the Law beftows upon a Wife.
Benevolence for Lawyers various fpeak ;
Some fay is once a month, fome once a week ;
However, from the whole, it doth appear,
One fhould not put it off beyond the year.
I own there is another fentiment,
That once in a whole life-time is fufficient.
Benevolence, fay thefe puzzlers and confounders,
Is juft the fame as riding of the bounders.
EMANUEL, quoth fhe, I cannot guefs,
Whether your Modefty or Wit is lefs ;
Wit, in a Mercer, is both fin and fhame ;
Return it to the ftews from whence it came---
I value not, quoth he, your wipes a ftraw---
I find great ufe in ftudying of the Law :
And now obferve---To all and fingular,
EMANUEL COOPER hereby doth declare,

By

By virtue of Recovery and Surrender,
It is agreed, between him and his Member,
That he, the faid EMANUEL, fhall direct,
And, for the future, fhew him no refpect;
And he, the faid EMANUEL, doth difclaim
All further finfull knowledge of his Dame,
In any fafhion, or in any place,
At any time or upon any cafe: ,
Provided, and it is hereby agreed,
If he and fhe to marrying accede,
This fhall by no means hinder the good man,
Then and at all times, to perform the beft he can —
    This crafty Covenant between thefe twain,
Hath made the Wedo think 'till thinking's vain;
And finding now no hope on other fcore,
Refolves at once, and doubteth nivir more---
Calleth her friends, maketh for life the leafe,
And fleepeth with EMANUEL in peace;
And, to compleat his and the Onkil's joy,
Bringeth him once a year a curios boy;
And now the Onkil's dead, and they have all,
And keep their Chriftenmafs at Cowper-Hall.

# P * * TY'S TALE;

## OR, THE

# CAVALIER NUN.

*Novimus et qui te, tranfverfa tuentibus hircis,*
*Et quo fed faciles nymphæ rifere facello.*

## TALE VII.

BOTH high and low! fimple and wife!
 Agree in making a great buftle,
About a certain pair of eyes,
 Belonging the Houfe of R----L.

Though not fo awful and difcreet,
 There was a pair of eyes at Brüffels,
Far more compaffionately fweet,
 Than Lady CAROLINA.R----L's.

Her eyes are like thofe fwords of fire,
 The flaming fwords to Angels given,
By which impure and rafh defire
 From the forbidden fruit are driven.

Far other eyes are thofe I mean,
 I fpeak of an inviting pair,
The property of frail eighteen,
 A Nun as amorous as fair.

Impaffion'd

Impaſſion'd eyes, fit for a Nun ;
  Eyes that love lights and VENUS ſhapes;
Eyes like the gilding of the ſun,
  Gilding ripe nectarines and grapes.

The Lady Abbeſs was her Aunt,
  And, as they lay in the ſame cell,
The Abbeſs was ſo complaiſant,
  She paſs'd her time exceeding well.

She had the privilege alone
  Of running in the convent-ground,
Surrounded by high walls of ſtone,
  Juſt like a filly in a pound.

Within this cloſe were ſhady trees,
  And there an Oratory ſtood ;
A Chapel of delight and eaſe,
  When folks delight in doing good.

After her matines and her complines,
  Here ſhe ſpent many pleaſant hours ;
Inſtead of making cakes and dumplings,
  Purſes and artificial flowers.

'Twas a delightful life ſhe led,
  Here every day ſhe met her monk,
Unleſs he was confin'd in bed,
  Which was the caſe when he was drunk.

                                        One

One day within this Oratory,
  As fhe was with her Monk in chat,
Inftead of being folitary,
  And melancholy as a cat;

Chatt'ring with many a lewd device,
  In which they neither were to feek,
Tricks that Love teaches in a trice,
  Better than ftudying a week;

In gibberifh, and playful cant,
  Father, fays fhe, pulling him down,
I've a great mind to turn gallant,
  And give your Reverence a green gown:

And, like my Aunt, I'll make you mad,
  As mad as King NEBUCHADNAZOR,
When fhe transforms you to a pad,
  As he was turn'd into a grazier.

For all your ftiffnefs and your pride,
  With whip and fpur, I'll make you run;
To which the humbled Monk reply'd,
  Spoufe of the Lord, thy will be done.

Her pad, as fturdy as a Miller's,
  She taught to rear, curvet, and prance,
  Make graceful caprioles, and dance,
As if he was between the pillars.

O                      The

The Nun cry'd out, My Lady Abbefs!
　My Lady Abbefs! without ceafe,
Your ways are ways of pleafantnefs,
　And all your paths are joy and peace.

———

This whole Tale is comprized in a fingle Monkifh diftich, which the Author has, with infinite delight, often heard repeated by the perfon whofe name this Tale bears. As the Tale is entirely taken from that hint, his worthy friend has the beft title to it.

*In viridi prato Monialem ludere vidi*
*Cum Monacho leviter, ille fub illa fuper.*

# Don PRINGELLO'S TALE:

## The FELLOWSHIP of the Holy NUNS;

### OR, THE

# MONK'S wife JUDGMENT.

## TALE VIII.

-------------------- *Detur potiori.*

Don PRINGELLO was a celebrated Spanish Architect, of
unbounded generosity; at his own expence, on the other
side of the Pyrenean mountains, he built many noble
castles, both for private people, and for the *public*, out
of his own funds; he repaired several palaces, situated
upon the pleasant banks of that delightful river, the
Garonne, in France, and came over on purpose to rebuild
Crazy Castle; but, struck with its venerable remains, he
could only be prevailed upon to add a few ornaments,
suitable to the stile and taste of the age it was built in.

THERE is a noble town call'd Ghent,
 A city, famous for its wares,
 For Priests and Nuns, and Flanders mares,
And for the best of fish in Lent.

There you may see, threat'ning destruction,
 A hundred forts and strong redoubts,
 Just like VAUBAN's, with in's and out's,
And cover'd-ways of love's construction.

       In

In one constructed as above,
   There dwelt two Nuns of the same age,
   Join'd like two birds in the same cage,
Both by necessity and love.

In towns of idleness and sloth,
   Where the chief trade is tittle-tattle,
   Tho' Priests are commoner than cattle,
They had but one between them both.

Our Nuns should have had two at least,
   In Ghent they're common as great guns,
   Which made it hard upon our Nuns,
And harder still upon the Priest.

But he was worthy of all praise,
   With spreading shoulders and a chest,
   A leg, a chine, and all the rest,
Like HERCULES of the FARNESE.

Amongst the Nuns there was a notion,
   That these two Sisters were assign'd,
   To him, for a severer kind
Of penitential devotion.

His penance lasted a whole year,
   And he had such a piece of work,
   If it had been for turning Turk,
It could not have been more severe.

                           Our

Our Nuns, which is no common cafe,
  Living together without jangling,
  All on a fudden fell a wrangling
About precedency and place.

They both with fpleen were like to burft,
  Like two proud Miffes when they fight,
  At an Affembly for the right,
Of being taken out the firft.

Before the Prieft they made this clatter,
  Between them both he was perplex'd,
  And ftudy'd to find out a Text
To end the controverted matter.

Children, faid he, fcratching his fconce,
  I fhould be better pleas'd than you,
  Could I divide myfelf in two,
And fatisfy you both at once.

Angels, perhaps, may have fuch powers,
  But it is fit and feafonable
  That you fhould be more reafonable,
Whilft you're with Beings fuch as ours.

Be friends, and liften to the Teacher,
  Ceafe your vain clamour and difpute,
  Be ye like little fifhes mute,
Before Saint ANTHONY the Preacher.

To

## Don PRINGELLO'S TALE.

To end at once all difputation,
  I'll fet my back againft that gate,
  And there produce, erect and ftraight,
The caufe of all your altercation.

But firft you both fhall hooded be,
  Both, fo effectually blinded,
  'Twill be impoffible to find it,
Except by Chance or Sympathy.

Which of you firft, be it agreed,
  The rudder of the Church can feize,
  Like PETER's Vicar with his keys,
Shall keep the helm, and have the lead;
  She fhall go firft, I mean to fay,
  . And have precedence every day.

The Nuns were tickled with the jeft,
  They were content, and he contriv'd
  To give the helm for which they ftriv'd,
To her that manag'd it the beft.

THE

# THE POET'S TALE;

## OR, THE

# CAUTIOUS BRIDE.

### TALE IX.

BRIDES, in all countries, have been reckon'd,
 For the firſt night, timid and cooliſh,
If they continue ſo the ſecond,
 They always have been reckon'd fooliſh ;

The reaſon's obvious and plain,
 In many nice and tickliſh caſes,
There's much to loſe and nought to gain,
 By affectation and grimaces.

A Bridegroom on the ſecond night,
 Whipt off the bedcloaths in ſurprize,
Behold, my dear, ſaid he, a ſight,
 Enough to make your choler riſe.

She turn'd away as red as ſcarlet,
 Whilſt he continu'd, Pray behold,
Lay hands on that outragious varlet,
 That looks ſo impudent and bold.

This is the fifteenth time in vain,
 He has been ſent to jail and fettered,
But there's no priſon can contain
 A priſon-breaker like JACK SHEPHERD.

The

The Bride turn'd round, and took her place,
    After fome ftudying and thinking,
Said fhe, recovering her face,
    Tho' modefty ftill kept her winking,

In vain the vagabond's committed,
    And to hard work and labour fent,
If you, his keeper, are outwitted
    By his pretending to repent;

You treat him ruggedly and hard,
    Whilft any infolence appears,
But you're difarm'd, and off your guard,
    The moment that he falls in tears.

Now you muft know, that I fufpect,
    A fellow-feeling in fome fhape,
Or elfe you would not through neglect,
    Let him continually efcape.

I'll lend no hand, unlefs you'll fwear,
    That you'll-deliver him to me,
And fuffer me to keep him there,
    'Till I confent to fet him free.

THE

# THE

# GOVERNOR of T**LBURY's TALE;

## OR, THE

# Unreafonable COMPLAINT.

### TALE X.

A Brute, a Peafant dwelt near Nantz,
  For they're fynonimous in France,
Who every day of his vile life,
When he had nothing elfe to do,
Thrafh'd, or apply'd his wooden fhoe,
  To the pofteriors of his wife:

But as all good and evil's equal,
All was balanc'd in the fequel;
  Every night, he had that pride;
His debit, on the whole amount
Of the pofterior account
  Was balanc'd by the other fide.

Like debts of honour loft at play,
Before he flept, he was fure to pay.
  And every morn before he rofe,
He left her over and above
A token of his conftant love,
  Steady and conftant as his blows.

P                                      One

One morning at his Spoufe's levee,
The blows and curfes fell fo heavy,
 Before the Lady of the place,
Poor JAQUETTE ran with her complaint,
With all the red and purple paint
 Beftow'd upon her nofe and face.

The Lady pity'd her juft grief,
And took a courfe for her relief;
 PIERRE was fummon'd to appear,
And muft have rotted in a jail,
Had he not found fufficient bail,
 For his behaviour for a year.

The dread of fines, a jail and whipping,
Like other folks, kept him from tripping.
 About a month after this pafs'd,
For JAQUETTE the good Lady fent,
And afk'd her if fhe was content,
 And PIERRE peaceable at laft.

Truly, fays fhe, I muft confefs,
That mine's a fingular diftrefs,
 For tho' he beat me black and blue;
At night he always made it up,
In bed, over a chearful cup,
 Where I was as content as you.

But

But now, he fays, he's off his mettle,
Becaufe we've no accounts to fettle.
   Let him indulge his appetite,
This very day let him begin
A frefh account, upon my fkin,
   And fettle it this very night.

After fuch plenty of good fare,
To be reduc'd is hard to bear.
   What then, my Lady, muft I feel,
Depriv'd entirely of my meat,
Without a morfel left to eat,
   Except what I can beg or fteal?

The Lady cry'd, You'd make one think,
That you did nought but eat and drink.
   Did you live always at this pafs,
Or now and then, and then it ceas'd,
Like Shrovetide, or a village Feaft,
   Or like a Bifhop's faying Mafs?

A tear ftood trembling in her eye,
Whilft JAQUETTE made her this reply.
   He was as fure as the Church Chimes!
And I can fay, what few can fay,
He allow'd me three warm meals a day,
   And afternoonings too fometimes.

P 2

'Twas

'Twas not from indigeftion,
That never was the queftion;
  If now and then my fare was worfe,
It was, becaufe the day before,
He happen'd to allow me more,
  Than was convenient for his purfe.

The Lady cry'd, fubmit in quiet,
  My Spoufe all day fhall thrafh his fill,
  I'll never fay that I'm us'd ill,
If he'll allow me fuch a diet,

# THE
# NOBLE REVENGE:
## OR THE
# L**B's TALE;

### TALE XI.

ALL people, languages, and nations,
  In fummer-time, have country ftations,
And have contrivances and ways,
Some very old and others new,
  To get the better of long days,
Which are the hardeft to fubdue.

In Italy the morning paffes
In vifiting and hearing maffes,
  And every creature, after dinner,
Retire in couples or alone,
  Both male and female, faint and finner,
Strip themfelves naked as a ftone.

All the world's out when night approaches,
A-foot, in curricles, and coaches;
  Then they give concerts and act plays,
And Sup at one another's houfes,
  The Wives go with their Chechifbays,
Their Mates with other people's Spoufes.

In France, and probably in Spain,
Summer gets on with toil and pain;
  The Ladies fally, with long canes,
To gather flowers, or pick a fallet,
  Attended by fantaftick Swains,
Like Figure-dancers in a ballet.

Some ftay within and do much better;
Some only ftay to write a letter;
  Others into the garden-run,
To bowl, or fhoot with bows and arrows;
  STREPHON, with CHLOE and a gun,
Makes love, and fires among the fparrows.
Kill all the tenants of the grove,
But let thofe live that only live to love.

Pray, how do Englifh fummers go?
They pafs their fummers but fo fo;
  More like the Germans than the French,
Drinking as long as they are able,
  And never thinking of a Wench,
'Till all the liquor's off the table:

But when they give their mind that way,
No people more alert than they.
  VENUS is cruelly afraid,
BACCHUS encroaches there fo much,
  Left he fhould fpoil the Cyprian trade,
As PLUTUS fpoils it with the Dutch.

One

One fummer, in the month of June,
My Lady was quite out of tune;
  To fet things right, fhe and my Lord
Repair to the old country-feat,
  Which to enjoy, with one accord,
They lie apart, and feldom meet.

They neither need to mope alone,
Each have companions of their own;
  His are the worft without all queftion,
Led-Captains, Squires, Parfons, without end;
  Hers, females of a ftrong digeftion,
Mingotti and her Fiddling Friends.

But then my Lord had a refource,
Which made things equaller of courfe:
  There is a place his Lordfhip chufes,
I know not upon what pretence,
  To call the Temple of the Mufes,
Built with lefs judgment than expence.

To pufh on time a little fafter,
My Lord appointing a toaft-mafter,
  Oft to the Temple's facred fhade,
Retires, like Numa to his charmer,
  To meet fome favourite Chamber-maid,
Or the fair Daughter of fome Farmer.

One

One afternoon a fpy reveal'd
The fecrets that thofe walls conceal'd---
  When my Lord was inclin'd to take it,
There was a room for making tea,
  My Lady's woman us'd to make it,
And always us'd to keep the key.

He had left off tea fome time; but why,
ABIGAIL was refolv'd to fpy.
  Within the room fhe made, or found,
A hole to peep into the next;
  Her labour with fuccefs was crown'd,
Though the difcovery made her vex'd.

He left off tea, you may infer,
Becaufe he was tir'd to death of her.
  She faw as plain as eyes could fee,
And never faw him half fo keen,
  My Lord as bufy as a bee,
Sipping the fweets of fweet Eighteen.

To be difcarded and turn'd off,
Of every fervant-wench the fcoff,
  For whom? The Wife of a mean Taylor:
Such was the Nymph in the Mufes houfe;
  She look'd as if fhe could impale her,
Even as a Taylor would a loufe.

My Lord return'd, fated with glory,
And BETTY ran to tell her ftory---
  Says fhe, your Ladyfhip's fo kind,
My zeal for you made me fufpicious;
  I watch'd, but never thought to find
Any thing downright flagitious.

Againft mankind fhe declaim'd next,
And then ftuck clofely to her text;
  Minutely painted the whole fcene,
The Nymph, her Age, her lovely Figure;
  And, to encreafe her Lady's fpleen,
She magnify'd his Lordfhip's vigour.

Great was her Ladyfhip's diftrefs,
How fhe would act, is hard to guefs;
  All folks allow Revenge is fweet,
And many think that nothing's fweeter,
  But 'tis a maxim with the Great,
  The meaner the Revenge the greater.

Caprice, according to FONTAINE;
Guides almoft every female brain;
  If meer caprice can raife a flame,
To make a Dwarf enjoy a Queen,
  Revenge, may make the nobleft Dame
Employ an inftrument as mean.

Nature left to herfelf moft prone is,
To follow the *Lex talionis,*

Q

In

In every nice and doubtful cafe,
My Lady drove as nature led ;
    And fo fhe took in my Lord's place,
Her rival's Hufband to her bed.

A Taylor's nothing on his board,
In bed he's better than a Lord,
    Her Ladyfhip found him fo there,;
And by his help, after ten years,
    At laft produc'd a Son and Heir,
That made my Lord the happieft of Peers.

## To the L A D I E S.

LADIES you have heard of Tit for Tat,---
Lex Talionis was like that:
    It was an equitable law, whereby
You weigh'd the perfon and the failure ;
    It gave you tooth for tooth, and eye for eye,
And for a Lord, fometimes a Taylor.

F  I  N  I  S.

# CONTENTS.

www.ingramcontent.com/pod-product-compliance
Lightning Source LLC
Chambersburg PA
CBHW032016010726

47493CB00007B/2427